Waiting

For

Empathy

By

Kenan Hudaverdi

Edited

By

Leslie Burns Angelocci

(Waiting for Empathy)

Copyright © 2019 by (Kenan Hudaverdi)

ISBN (XXXXXXXXXXXX)

Table of Contents

Chapter 1 6

Chapter 2 11

Chapter 3 30

Chapter 4 46

Chapter 5 68

Chapter 6 79

Chapter 7 91

Chapter 8 103

Chapter 9 118

Chapter 10 134

Chapter 11 140

Chapter 12 149

Chapter 13..158

Chapter 14.. 165

Chapter 15 174

Chapter 16.. 184

Chapter 17... 198

Chapter 18 202

Chapter 19 219

Chapter One

Moving to a New House

Eva is a very attractive sixty-five-year-old woman slim with blond hair and blue eyes, her home is just six and a half miles from Brighton in East Sussex in a little town called Peacehaven. Not far from the white cliffs on the coast, and on a stretch of green grass that runs along the promenade, this one-story bungalow has been Eva's home for the past twenty-five years.

This precious little home is the second home from the corner on Bayview Road; the house next door to her had been for sale for a year and was recently sold to a man who was in a hurry to move in. Eva and the gentleman had not yet spoken when she saw him unloading and carrying furniture into the home next door.

Fifteen years ago, Eva's husband passed away from a heart attack, they'd been married for twenty-five years at the time. To the outside world, the two looked as if they had the "perfect marriage".

During the twenty-five years, there were no children for the couple so, when her husband passed away Eva was alone with no family of her own and no family on her husband's side as well.

Left all alone in the world apart from her little white dog Kimmy. Eva lived a solitary life with her dog as her constant companion.

Across from the house is a patch of grass that runs along the white clifftops and there in front of her house, is a bench that could seat two people whilst looking out to Friar's Bay. The sea stretched for miles across the English Channel, the view is beautiful and endless.
Under the white cliffs, there is a long walkway that can be reached by a staircase, local folks and tourists found this to be a great place for bike riding, hiking, and walking dogs.

After losing her husband, Eva became depressed and reclusive only leaving the house when she needed to get a few things.
She would spend her days and evenings, cleaning and watching TV and taking Kimmy out for walks above the cliffs or sometimes they would walk down under the cliffs, along the walkway.

George Williams is moving in next door to Eva, he's a sixty-four-year-old man who would rather laugh and joke than be serious.

George is a professional boxing trainer. Long ago, in his early life he was a professional boxer himself and after retiring, he turned his knowledge and skills to training fighters.

Over the past thirty-five years George had produced fifteen World Champions ranging from Flyweight, to Heavyweight. George is a no-nonsense trainer when it comes to his fighters. Clearly, he was taken seriously by all that knew of him when he was inducted into the International Boxing Hall of Fame three years ago in 2016, and was knighted in the same year by the Queen, for "Services to Sport."

Twenty-two years ago, one of George's fighters, Brendan Murphy a World Champion was fighting to defend his seventh title, in that fight Brendan hit his opponent with such force that he died in the ring. It was the referee's fault as he should have stopped the fight long before the opponent hit the canvas, but by then it was too late. Brendan was devastated.

Brendan Murphy never laced on another pair of boxing gloves after the tragedy. Brendan had made a great deal of money from boxing and was wise enough to invest his money in various things, one being property, another was a gym where kids of all ages could come and get off the streets, get focused and be trained by George and Brendan as well as many other coaches. The community business owners were happy to become sponsors for the gym to help ensure that the kids and adults in the area would benefit from such a generous commitment by Brendan.

With social media and cyber bullying, kids often turn to the streets, Brendan and George both knew this and were more than enthusiastic about helping the youth in the community and also providing a safe haven for all the members of the community that were interested in staying in shape and making their lives better.

Brendan lives with his wife Eileen in a large home just outside Brighton that has several acres of land. Eileen stood by Brendan through thick and thin. Together, they have one son, Liam who also has his own house on the property, as do many animals such as chicken's, dogs, cats, some young sheep.

Liam is married to his school sweetheart Fiona. The two met in secondary school they have been together for ten years and married for six years. Blessed with two beautiful girls, the oldest is five her name is Kate and the younger is Sophia who is three years old.

Since giving birth, Fiona's weight has ballooned to twelve stones. Being short in stature, her weight and height combined makes her look rather large, but Liam could care less; he's madly in love with her and adores her and the two children. He is so much like his father, a gentleman in private, a fierce competitor in the ring.

Liam is a very strong headed individual; much like his father, despite all of Brendan's efforts to keep Liam from boxing, the kid was a natural. Liam had spent his life watching his dad and as a young boy began boxing; out of 130 amateur fights, he had only been defeated three times and was never knocked out nor had he never visited the canvas. Liam was his father's son, with the tender heart of his mother Eileen.

Brendan is Liam's manager as well as, a Television boxing commentator. Fiona is Liam's publicist but is never seen by the ring side. When Fiona saw him fight, she became overwhelmed and has refused to be ringside since Liam became a professional boxer.

Eileen is in charge of the house it is there she is the boss as it has always been. She has help from a gentleman named Jack who helps with the gardens along with his wife Claire who is the housekeeper. The two have worked for the family for twenty-five years and are very much a part of the family. Eileen also cares for her two granddaughters. Although nearly impossible, she tries not to spoil the children, but every now and again, she has grandmother's rights. Eileen looks to George much like a father figure; she loves and respects George as he has stood by her family through everything over the years.

George had been training Liam, who is fighting for a "Middleweight Eliminator" in two months' time at London's "O2 Arena". It's a huge fight as the arena holds twenty thousand people, and the tickets for the fight are already sold out. Liam is one fight away from fighting for the "World Title".

George has had his own room at the family house since the days of Brendan's "World Champion" career. He is also godfather to Liam, and both of his girls Kate and Sofia.

Longing for a permanent home for himself, George made the move to buy the house by the sea. George loves the sea and the tranquility of being near it; he's found the perfect place for himself on the quiet street upon the cliffs.

Chapter Two

George and Eva's First Meeting

After all the boxes and furniture were moved into his new home, George made himself a mug of tea. The fog was lifting off the sea as George stepped outside and across the road to the bench. George thought quietly about the brilliant view as he gazed upon the little boats revealed to him as the fog lifted, George was feeling very contented when suddenly, Kimmy appeared.

Kimmy, is a Maltese pup that approached George with her tail wagging happily. Kimmy began sniffing at George's feet. Playfully, George starts talking with the dog and petting her.

"Do you want some loving huh? Oh yes, you want some loving yeah!"

Kimmy was responding to George's playful words jumping back and then dashing forward with excitement.

Due to her age Kimmy was slower than most, she is showing signs of slowing down so George figures she must be an older pup.

George sensed someone next to him. Looking upwards he sees Eva standing there watching, she looks to be six feet tall.

"Good Morning!"

Eva looks sad and withdrawn yet so beautiful with her blond hair and her beautiful blue eyes.

"Good Morning, apologies to you, she is not usually this friendly with people she doesn't know."

"What's her name?"

"Kimmy."

"How old is she?"

"She's fourteen. She has not been feeling well so, I took her to the vets yesterday. I will go back tomorrow to find out the results of her tests."

George looks at Eva for a second taking in her beauty.

"My name is George, George Williams. I just moved into the corner house over the past couple of days.

"Very nice to meet you George, my name is Eva, Eva Hudson. I live next door to you."

"The kettle is still hot; I could bring you a cup of tea or coffee out if you'd like to join me."

"No thank you."

"It will only take a few minutes."

"No, I'm fine. Thank you for the offer. Perhaps, next time?"

"Are you married?"

"Mr. Williams, are you always this forward with the people you meet for the first time?"

"Yes!"

"I am a widow. My husband passed away right where you are sitting."

George gets to his feet swiftly.

"My condolences for your loss."

"Thank you, Mr. Williams."

"You can call me George. How old are you?"

"Mr. Williams, no gentleman would ever ask a lady her age!"

"I don't have those rules in my book."

"I can see that!"

"How tall are you? You must be at least six foot tall!"

"Mr. Williams!"

"Yes!"

"It's evident that I'm much taller than you, and as you thought, I am indeed six feet tall."

"You are beautiful!"

"Mr. Williams, are you trying to embarrass me?"

"No. I am paying you a compliment. It appears to me that it's been such a long time since you had a compliment that you don't know how to respond. A simple thank you will do."

Eva tries to compose herself. She is now unsettled and tries to explain while composing herself.

"Mr. Williams, your line of questioning and curiosity has taken me by a surprise. It's true, I have not had a compliment in years, but then again, I never go looking for one and never put myself in a situation where I would receive one. Now that we are neighbors, I accept your compliment and thank you sincerely."

"How about dinner one night in town?"

"No. I don't think it's a good idea. We live next door to each other."

"And... The moral of the story is?"

"Mr. Williams, it's been nice to meet you. Have a good day."

Eva turns away and begins to walk followed by Kimmy. George calls to her.

"Eva!"

"There is a condition attached if you have dinner with me."

Eva looks frustrated and walks back to George.

"What are the conditions of going out to dinner with you? If you say that I'd have to sleep with you, I'll punch you so hard that you will fly across the channel like a missile, and then skid on your ass in France!"

Suddenly, Eva begins to hyper ventilate, struggling to breathe, George jumps to his feet.

"What's wrong with you? Do you have asthma?"

"Eva shakes her head no."

"Are you having a panic attack?"

"Yes, yes." (She continues to gasp for air)

"Alright then, listen to me and do as I ask you to, it will be fine."

Eva does not respond. Finally, she nods her head.

"Listen carefully, I want you to take a deep breath and count to four as you breathe in, then hold for one second, exhale to four, and hold for a second. Repeat this until I tell you to stop ok? Now stand straight and place both your hands on my shoulders."

She nods her head, stands straight, and she places her hands-on George's shoulders. Taking a huge breath in, George is counting, "One, two, three, and four. Eva exhales. "One, two, three, four." Eva holds for a second and then repeats the process. The more she repeats, the calmer she becomes. George is looking at the color in her face and her slower breathing pattern; she's much, much better and calmer. Eva is breathing normally now.

"Come and sit down for a few moments and relax."

Eva sits down with Kimmy at her feet. She gazes out to the sea.

"I've never met a man that could make me so mad in the first few minutes of meeting him. You Mr. Williams have broken a record!"

"I'm sorry. I don't know why you would get so mad! I didn't say anything bad or ugly to you. The condition I had in mind was that, you wear high heels, not to sleep with me, but since it crossed your mind."

Eva stands straight to her feet and looks down on him.

"Mr. Williams it's a definite No to dinner! No to high heels, and definitely; No to sleeping with you! Have a pleasant day."

"No problem."

George is watching her as she walks away on the grass parallel to the road that leads away from their houses.

That evening George is in his front room, there are boxes everywhere that need to be sorted out and things to be put away. George had just made a cup of coffee and was looking around his new home when the doorbell rang. Thinking wondered who would be ringing his bell. Opening the door, there is Eva.

"Hi there!"

"Mr. Williams, I had a good think about what happened today, I was in the wrong. I've come to extend my apology to you."

"Well, no self-respecting man would ever accept an apology from a lady at the door, please do come in."

"Mr. Williams, I don't think I should."

"Hey, this is my home, and you are my neighbor, as well as the first to ring my bell, and my first guest since I've moved in. Tomorrow there's going to be bedlam here with the house full of people to help sort all this stuff out. Please do come in!"

"Since you put it like that, I accept, but please understand that I cannot stay long."

"Well alright. I hope you'll stay long enough for tea or coffee and for Kimmy to have some water."

Eva enters into the open living area of the house; its filled boxes and misplaced furniture. George makes his way to the kitchen.

"I'll get some water for Kimmy."

"Thank you."

"What about you? Tea or coffee?"

"Tea please, with milk if you don't mind."

"Sure. Make yourself at home; the place is upside down for the time being but it will all get sorted out tomorrow. One never knows how much junk they own until they move.

I had a room at my friend's house for over twenty years, most of this stuff was in storage but I moved it all here in one place, it's much better this way."

George turns on the kettle and places some fresh water in a bowl for Kimmy. George places the bowl on the floor and Kimmy scurries over to lap up some refreshing water.

"You're thirsty huh? Yeah! Drink your water and you will get some loving if you are a good, as you can see little one, the place is upside down, so please no peeing in the house or I will bust your nose wee one."

Eva watches and listens to George talking with the dog. Her eyes smile as she tries to stay composed and muster up the courage to begin a conversation with him.

"As I was saying at the door, I came to apologize."

"There's no need for an apology."

"Why not?"

"Because I can't imagine anyone staying angry with me for too long. You're here because there was nothing to be angry about in the first-place, right?"

"Who are you Mr. Williams?"

"I'm someone you want in your corner when things get tough, when you need a friend the most."

George hands Eva her tea "Please come and have a seat."

The settee is right in the middle of the room with the armchairs on either side. Eva sits in one of the armchairs with her tea and takes a sip appearing obviously uncomfortable.

George sits across from her and looks at her so intensely that it feels as though he's looking into her soul. Eva can't help but notice this and lowers her eyes, taking another sip of her tea.

"Are you retired Mr. Williams?"

"No. I have one of those jobs I can do till I am eighty years old if I live that long."

"So, what is it that you do that allows you to work till you are eighty years old?"

"I make history."

"You make history?"

"Yeah! I make history."

"How do you do that?"

"I'm a boxing trainer. I produce World Champions!"

"I don't like boxing. It's so brutal. Two men in a square ring, bash each other's faces into bloody messes, I find it repugnant."

"Boxing is more than two men beating each other's faces in; it is an art form! It requires dedication, focus, hard work, and many years to develop the skills to be a world champion. Two fighters fighting for the "World Title" is equivalent to what the romans used to call "Gladiators". The difference is, boxers don't use swords, and don't fight to the death. Although throughout the history of boxing there have been some fatalities in the ring."

"I think they should ban boxing if it's such a dangerous sport!"

"The most dangerous sport in the world is not boxing."

"I cannot imagine another sport more dangerous then boxing. You must be pulling my leg Mr. Williams."

"No, no, I'm not! I mean it! It is not boxing!"

"Ok then, what's the most dangerous sport in the world?"

"It's a sport that does not have contact with another person and yet, more people die doing it than any other sport in the world."

"I've never heard so much rubbish in all my life Mr. Williams! How can a sport be the most dangerous sport in the world where more people die from it then boxing, and yet, there is no contact with another person? Now, you are really pulling my leg!"

"No, it's true, in fact more people die from the sport I'm talking about then all the other physical sports put together."

"That's impossible!"

"Only to someone who does not know it's possible. Truly, the most dangerous sport in the world, is fishing."

"I thought fishing was a past time, not a sport."

"Oh, it's a sport! People have all kinds of difficulties and they cannot save themselves. They end up drowning. Sometimes, they fall on the rocks and bang their head, then the tide carries them away. Sometimes while on a small boat, things go very wrong. There is a great saying about the sea, and I quote; "Any man who is not afraid of God let him go to sea."

"I love the sea. I love the sound of the waves here at night. I leave my window ajar at night so that I can listen to the waves while I fall asleep."

"Can I ask you a question Eva?"

"It depends on how personal it is. I might not answer it and you might infuriate me again. So, Mr. Williams, choose your words carefully."

"Do you suffer from depression?"

Eva looks at him for a few seconds and nods her head in defeat and replies; "Yes. How did you know?"

"The panic attacks. I knew someone who had a nervous breakdown and he would often have panic attacks like you did. It happened when he was stressed about something. The panic attacks have passed and he is alright now, you could say he's as good as new."

"I'm too sensitive to the world and any kind of cruelty to animals or people. Arrogant, and insensitive people, can set me off as well. I am sorry. I did not come here to dump all my problems on you."

"It's ok. I'm a professional dumping ground for problems because people trust and confide in me. Those that do, know that what we speak about will stay with me until the grave. I have had that effect on people from an early age."

"Thank you for your hospitality. Thank you for the tea and the water for Kimmy. I better go now."

Eva hands over the cup to George.

"I have some friends coming over tomorrow to help with moving some of this stuff around and putting everything where it belongs. In the evening, we are going to have a house warming party outside on the grass by the bench. There will be a BBQ and a mass of other assorted goodies like wine and a little music. I'd very much like for you to join us Eva."

"I don't think it's a good idea."

"The whole world is built on good ideas and here's you slowly putting a stop to human progress by creating a whole new thing called "I don't think it's a good idea syndrome." Just say yes. You will have a great time. All of my friends are crazy like me! You will adore them, and they will adore you!"

"I must say Mr. Williams, you are full of self-confidence! Is this some kind of bravado and machismo on your part to impress me?"

"It would be an insult to your beauty and your intelligence if I used such tactics to get a yes out of you! It's more of a "neighborly request" to have the pleasure of your company."

"Where did you learn to speak like that? I have never heard anyone speak like you."

"Is it such a bad thing, the way I speak?

"I don't know if you are really intelligent or just crazy."

"Maybe, I'm just punch drunk. I know a broken soul, when I see one, I see that in you. Tragically, most people die young in life and aren't buried until they are old. I know in that broken soul of yours lives a beautiful, sensitive woman, with an abundance of elegance, beauty, and charm."

Eva cannot believe what she has just heard; she looks at George a bit shocked at his eloquence.

"Mr. Williams, no one has ever said such beautiful words to me before. How do you know all this about me? Are you guessing, or do you really know? If you do know, I want to know how you know."

"The truth is, I know it's a fact, otherwise I would not waste my breath saying it to you. The complicated part is I don't know myself how I know, except that I do know. That's the truth! Will you come?"

"Yes."

"Good!"

"Mr. Williams, I'm very weary of people. I don't trust easy, because most people talk a lot of shit most of the time and I don't have patience for all of that. Do you understand?"

"Yes. I do understand. There is a simple answer to that, the next time someone talks a lot of shit to you, just ask them if their ass get jealous of all of the shit that comes out of their mouth."

"Mr. Williams, are you bipolar by any chance?"

"No, I am a Gemini!"

Eva shakes her head.

"Thank you for the tea I will see you tomorrow evening."

"Good luck at the vets tomorrow with Kimmy, I hope everything turns out well."

"Thank you. Good night."

"Good night."

George walks Eva to the door. She hesitates for a moment and looks at George.

"You might as well know I'm sixty-five years old."

"Well, I'm sixty-three years old. You're two years older than me, and with high heels on, you are one foot taller than me. We make a perfect couple!"

"Do you always turn everything into a joke and see the funny side of life? Are you ever serious?"

"When I need to be yes."

There is a long pause between them. Eva turns and walks away with Kimmy by her feet. Before she gets out of the gate, she feels that George is walking with her. She stops and he steps next to her with a cheeky grin.

"What are you doing?"

"I'm walking you home, it's dark. Don't you know anything can happen in the dark?"

"I live next door."

"I know. It will make me feel better knowing you got home safely."

"Oh, for goodness sake! I suppose I can't stop you!"

Within a few yards they've arrived outside Eva's house. George waits until Eva and Kimmy have stepped safely into the house. Exhaling a large, deep breath, he turns and heads over to the bench. The sound of the waves below the cliffs can be heard hitting the shoreline, the night sky is filled with sparkling stars that that glisten and dance in the dark. George is lost in deep thought as he casts his gaze out onto the sea.

Eva is in her front room at the window, she peeks out from behind the curtain to see George sitting on the bench. Watching him for just a few seconds, she then lets the curtain go and retreats to her bathroom to run a warm bath.

Chapter Three
Sorting Out the House

The next morning, Brendan and Eileen are the first to arrive at George's. George greets them at the door and the two enter as if they've always lived there. George had lived with them together for over twenty years as a family so this was all very natural for them. Eileen hugs George as always with a kiss on the cheek, then hands George a beautifully framed Irish blessing that she had brought him as a house warming gift.

"This is for your wall for everyone to see and read."

George takes it out of the wrapper and reads it.

"May your troubles be less and your blessings are more and nothing but happiness comes through your door, may your home be a place where friends meet family gathers and love grows."

"Thank you, Eileen. Please, would you find a place for it where you think it looks best?"

Eileen takes the framed blessing and begins looking around for the perfect spot.

After twenty minutes, Brendan and George are in the garden drinking tea and talking. Brendan looks at George.

"We have Jack and Claire coming to give us a hand today."

"You didn't have to do that Brendan."

"It wasn't my idea, it was Eileen's. Well, it was really Jack's idea.

"Jack is a good man Brendan."

"Yep, that he is! Those two are not just the gardener and house keeper, they are family."

"I knew you couldn't come up with an idea like that all by yourself. How are things between you and Eileen?"

"Great! Couldn't be better! She is worried about Liam though. Personally speaking, I did not want this fight for Liam; I think the guy is too dangerous. He's known as an animal in the ring."

"Liam will become the animal tamer in the ring. He is a good boxer with a great gift. I'm sure he will be a great fighter just like you used to be if he continues to listen to instructions and applies them. You had to learn to do the same and you turned out to be a Champion."

"It would kill us both if anything happened to him."

"Liam is my godson; it would kill me if anything happened to him. He is going to be in the best shape of his life for this fight mentally, physically, and emotionally. I will see to that!"

"I trust you George. You almost single handily have given us the lifestyle we are blessed with today because of your expertise. I have never ever thanked you properly for everything so, today, I am saying thank you."

"Will you get a grip? You're the one who had your nose busted, your eyes blackened, and ribs broken. It's you that has done all the hard work! You and your family deserve all the blessings in the world!"

"I will never forget all the good things you did for me even before I had my first fight. You encouraged me, gave me advice like a father figure even though you were young man yourself in those days training children in that old gym. Your kindness, and generosity, is known by everyone who has trained with you. I've never forgotten what you told me as a kid aspiring to be somebody in the world; that all fights are won in the gym, not in the ring. I never told you this before George, when you were knighted; it was one of the proudest moments of my life."

George looks at Brendan.

"Have you been sparring? Are you punch drunk this morning, coming out with all this melancholy stuff first thing?"

"I thought this was a good time and place to say these things to you so, that you don't think all your hard work, kindness, and generosity has been taken for granted or that I will ever forget what you've done for me and my family."

"It was a privilege working with you Champ! I'm very proud to have served as your trainer for all those years. I'm even more proud that you built a gym for the kids, to get them off the streets and away from gangs and drugs. Very proud indeed! With Liam training at the gym as a contender for a world title fight; it will give those kids inspiration, to aspire to be like you and Liam. It's a privilege working with Liam as well! Don't worry about the kid; he is going to be fantastic on fight night!"

Eileen shouts out from the back door into the garden.

"Are you two going to stand there all-day gossiping? We have work to do! Jack and Claire, Liam and the kids are here, and the mini bus is full of teenagers from the gym will be arriving quickly! We have work to do! Let's get cracking!"

Ten minutes later, the front room is full of people. Anyone from the outside would think there was military training going on. Eileen is in charge of everyone, telling them where everything should go.

"First things first, open all the boxes, clothes go upstairs to the bedroom, put them on the bed, books go over there on the wall shelf, kitchen utensils go in the kitchen where Claire will sort them out. Trophies and pictures leave them in that corner we will decide where they will go later. I want everything out of the boxes within one hour. All the empty boxes need to be folded and put into the shed in the garden. After all that is done, I'd like everyone to go home and come back tonight for the house warming party. Let's do this!"

Everyone in the room begins to work as a team. All the boxes are opened and the contents removed. Within an hour everything was out of the boxes and placed either in the kitchen, the bookshelves, or up in the bedroom. Once done, and as instructed all the boxes were folded and placed int garden shed.

Eva was nearly at her house after visiting the vets with Kimmy, wanting to tell George about the visit to the vets her thoughts were abruptly interrupted as she approached the front gate of the house. There were cars parked outside the houses also a she saw a mini bus with writing on the side that read; "Brendan's Boys Club Where Future Champions Are made."

A Lot of teenagers came out of the house and walked past Eva as she held Kimmy in her arms. The kids all pile into the mini bus and drive away.

Eva hesitantly moved towards the open front door and called out into the house.

"Mr. Williams?"

In the front room Eileen whispers under her breath to Fiona.

"Mr. Williams."

Fiona smiles and shrugs.

George walks to the front door and greets Eva.

"Hello. I hope you have good news about Kimmy."

"Yes, everything checked out fine. She's all good."

"Come on in."

"I don't want to intrude Mr. Williams."

"Come now; let me introduce you to my family."

Eva steps in and looks around. The house is clean and tidy with all the boxes out of the way. She stops a few feet into the living room, it appears that everyone is about to leave. George looks at Eva and smiles, then turns and introduces Eva to everyone.

"Friends and family, this is Eva my next- door neighbor and her sweet pup Kimmy. Eva, let me introduce you to Brendan, the former World Champion, his beautiful wife Eileen, over there is Jack, and his wife Claire, and this young lad, is the future "World Champion" Liam, and his beautiful wife, Fiona. The noise you're hearing upstairs is coming from Fiona and Liam's two gremlins, Kate and Sophie."

Eva quietly but politely responds.

"Nice to meet you all."

Eileen steps forward.

"We were just leaving to go and get some shopping for tonight's house warming party. I hope George has the good sense to invite you, and if he hasn't, I am now. We will see you tonight then Eva, so nice to meet you and Kimmy."

"Thank you, Eileen. It's very nice to meet you too!"

"Ok everyone, let's go!"

George interrupts Eileen's departure.

"Let me give you some money for the party shopping Eileen."

Brendan steps in quickly.

"Don't worry about that, we have that covered George!"

"I insist."

Eileen walks over to George and kisses him on the cheek.

"It's covered. See you tonight around seven."

George nods his head in humble appreciation, as the girls come running down the stairs. Kate runs to George and hugs him followed by Sophie. Kate looks up at George.

"Uncle George, Sophie wants to know if we can have one of the rooms for when we come to stay with you."

There is silent pause. Everyone looks at Kate and George.

"You don't have a room here."

Kate looks horribly disappointed.

"Oh no."

Sophie puts her head down in sadness.

"The house is yours."

Kate and Sophie lift their heads up in surprise and joy.

"Really?"

"Yes of course, on one condition, that you must both behave yourselves!

"We promise Uncle George we'll be good, honest, we will."

"And if you are not good?"

Suddenly, George grabs both girls by the shoulders with each hand like an iron claw gripping them gently and playfully. Both girls start to pretend to shake and shiver.

"Oh No! Not the wings, no, not the wings!"

Everyone in the room smiles at the sight of George playing with the girls.

"Ok then, that's settled. Your mum and dad can sort out one of the rooms for you two, and the other room for them. I will have my own room. If grandma and grandad come to stay, I will sleep downstairs."

Both girls nod their heads in happiness. George leans down and kisses each of them on the cheek.

"I'll see you tonight."

The girls pass in front of Eva.

"Nice meeting you, see you later tonight Miss Eva."

Liam and Fiona hug George and head out the door.

Kate stops and looks at Eva again.

"Are you Uncle George's girlfriend?"

Eva is somewhat embarrassed by the question.

"No."

"Kate I'm going bust your nose."

"Ops! Sorry Uncle George!"

Kate hurries out the door.

Jack steps forward with a grin.

"Well, we have finally gotten rid of you! I will bring over the oil drum BBQ for tonight and put it outside by the bench on the grass."

"How many people are you expecting to come to this house warming party?"

"Everyone we know, everyone you know, and some of the teenagers from the gym, with their parents as well. There may be a few other local people that support the gym joining us as well, don't worry there will be plenty of food and entertainment for everyone."

"I thought we were having a house warming party, it sounds like it's turned into a street carnival! I better give you some money for some drinks."

"We don't need anything. As Eileen said, it's all covered and the music is sixties and seventies to reflect your age. I'll see you around six tonight to spark up the BBQ."

Claire kisses George on the cheek.

"I will be over once a week to clean the house and get whatever you need from the market."

"I don't need a housekeeper Claire. I can look after myself."

"You have no choice. These are orders from Brendan and Eileen. Do you want to argue with Eileen?"

"God Forbid!" I will get a set of keys cut for you."

"Good! See you tonight!"

Jack and Claire stop in front of Eva.

"Nice to meet you Eva. We look forward to seeing you tonight."

They close the door behind them. There is a simple silence that is evidence that everyone is gone. Eva and George are alone.

"Can I offer you some tea or coffee?"

"No thank you. Everything looks organized, and wonderful."

"Thank you. So glad everything is good with Kimmy."

"Thank you. I almost forgot; I have something for you."

"You have something for me?"

Eva rummages through her bag and produces a brown bag with something small inside and hands it to George. Looking at Eva for a second he looks inside the bag and finds a small fridge magnet.

It is a quotation from Muhammed Ali.

"Friendship is the hardest thing in the world to explain. It's not something you learn in school. But if you haven't learned the meaning of friendship, you really haven't learned anything."
— Muhammad Ali

"It's just a small gift for your new home. I'm sure you admire Muhammed Ali."

Thank you. I do admire him Eva; he was a great man, in and out of the ring. Ali will always be the Greatest! Not only was he a Champion Boxer but he was also known for all the great charity work he did outside of the ring. Such an incredible human being. That's why I admire him and why he will always be the Greatest in my eyes."

"I agree. I must go now."

"I'll see you tonight?"

"I don't think it's a good idea Mr. Williams. I haven't been to a party in years."

"Well, that can all change with a simple yes."

"I won't know anyone at the party. I'm concerned I might end up having panic attack in the middle of all that and I don't want to spoil your evening."

"My evening will only be spoiled if you don't turn up."

"Why are you insisting I be here, Mr. Williams?"

"I like you, and honestly, I wouldn't feel right having a party and you are alone at home. As Muhammed Ali said, "Friendship is the hardest thing in the world to explain." I hope we can have the kind of friendship where instead of you saying; "it's not a good idea", you'll say, I think that's a great idea."

"I'm a shy person. I have been a recluse for years. I don't know if I can handle it."

"You will be my guest; all my friends will adore you. I know it's not easy for you but perhaps, me moving here, next door to you, was meant to be. Maybe there is a divine intervention taking place right now in our lives. Maybe, this is the work of the great universe and we were meant to meet and all of this was supposed to happen."

"Mr. Williams, do you actually believe in all that crap, about destiny and that there is a reason for us meeting, and living next door to each other?"

"The fact that it's true is evidence enough for me. Will you come tonight?"

"Yes."

"Ok good. What time will you be ready?"

"What do you mean what time I will be ready?"

"I want to know so that I can come and pick you up?"

"Mr. Williams, I am forty feet away from the bench outside. I think I can find my way."

"Yes, I know that. Every girl likes to be picked up from their house."

"You're going to come and pick me up?"

"Yes. Be ready for seven then, I will be there to pick you up."

"Ok."

"Ok."

"I have to go now. See you at seven."

"Ok."

Chapter Four

The BBQ

Right around five in the afternoon close friends began to
arrive at the house. Jack and Liam have the oil drum BBQ
placed directly across from the bench on the grass about five
feet away from the edge of the cliff. Brendan and a few other
guys from the gym started to set up the tables and chairs
into a line along the bench. Kate and Sophia have brought
along their little pink bikes and are busying themselves by
riding up and down the lane while the adults are getting
things set up.

Inside, Claire, Eileen, and Fiona have taken over the kitchen
organizing all the food. The ladies are joined by two young
men from the local butchers carrying huge trays of sausages,
lamb chops, steak, ribs, and chicken.

At six o'clock, Liam empties three bags of charcoal into the
BBQ drum, squirts some paraffin onto the charcoal and
lights it. This particular night was beautiful and clear;
perfect a housewarming party as the sun is hung above the
sea in the distance.

One of the guys stretched out a power cable that ran from
George's house, across the road towards far side of the

bench. A van arrived and several teenagers got out and began unloading portable electric lights that they carried to the grass. Everything had been though through, including being able to light the area where Liam would be tending the BBQ.

The other three kids were placing portable lights along the edge of the grass. The lights are telescopic so, the boys extended them high as they would go, making sure to point them towards the long table.

Shortly after the lights were in, the DJ arrived and began setting up his table and equipment. He was careful to make sure that all the cables and cords were covered and marked so that no one would trip over them during the festivities.

The time to go get Eva was approaching. George had showered and shaved and was applying aftershave. Next, he took out his pin stripped suit out of the closet and got dressed. Checking his watch, it's now five minutes until seven. Glancing in the mirror, George takes a deep breath and walks down to the kitchen where Claire is sorting the food and making trays. Claire looks up to see George looking very dapper.

"Try and be a good boy tonight George. Oh, and George, let's try and get through the night without any mishaps, shall we?"

"Where's Jack?"

"He's outside at the BBQ with some meat for Liam."

"I want you out there enjoying yourself tonight Claire. I don't want you spending the night in my kitchen! Understand?"

"Yes, and hey you better watch it George, my husband doesn't even tell me what to do, he knows better! By the way George, in my opinion, you look rather nice! Try and behave won't you!"

"I'll see you out there, I have to go."

George leaves the house. There's smoke coming from the BBQ, soft music playing, and people are starting to gather. More cars are arriving and dropping off guests then pulling around to park. Eileen, Fiona, Brandan, Jack, and Liam are chatting as another twenty or more people from the local community and businesses gather at the party.

George does not stop to speak; instead he heads straight to Eva's house. Eileen is watching with a grin on her face, she's noticed how carefully George has dressed and how he's walking; shoulders back and head up. George has his "date demeanor" on.

There is a local man named Kenny there, he's a big, burly man in stature, standing six foot, four inches tall, he's built like a house and looks like an overweight, heavyweight. Kenny owns the four-star "Sea View Hotel" and is a good friend of George and Brendan's family for years. Seeing George, Kenny calls out to him.

"George! Where you going you punch drunk mackerel? The party is over here!"

George stops and looks at Kenny. The two have always loved to insult each other in jest. George is happy to reply in turn.

"You'd better behave yourself tonight you ill-bred, ill-mannered uncivilized, uncouth, uncultured, mosquito!"

Kenny turns and looks at Brendan

"Brendan, George is talking to you."

Eileen is with Kenny's wife Jackie. Shaking her heads Jackie looks to Eileen.

"I'm still waiting for him to grow up!"

Eileen responds.

"After thirty years, you will need a miracle for that to happen! And while we are on the subject, I need one for Brendan also!"

As George approaches Eva's front door, he takes another deep breath and knocks several times, he straightens the collar of his suit while waiting. After a few moments, the door opens and Eva appears wearing a long white summer dress. Eva looks stunning. Very little make up on, her hair neatly done, she's a picture of beauty to George. They both look at each other for a few seconds. George is overwhelmed at just how lovely Eva looks. Breaking the silence and the look between them, Eva begins with a compliment.

"Mr. Williams, you look very nice in your suit."

"Thank you. I have to tell you that you look amazing! If you were my girl, I would say to you, let's forget about going out tonight and just go straight upstairs and make love."

"Mr. Williams!"

"Yes?"

"Do you still want me to come to this house warming party?"

"Yes!"

"Then you best behave yourself!"

"Ok! Let's go!"

Eva steps out of the door followed by Kimmy.

"Regarding the suit, in truth, it's the only one I have. This suit has served me well over the years. I've worn it to engagements, weddings, funerals, and maybe one day if I live long enough, I might even wear it at my own wedding. Right now, I think I have more of a chance of wearing it for my funeral, rather than at my wedding."

"Mr. Williams."

"Yes."

"Don't you ever run out of things to say?"

"Never! What fun would that be?"

They walk to the grass and George heads straight to Eileen and Jackie who are standing together enjoying a glass of wine. Eileen greets Eva, introduces her to Jackie and offers Eva refreshment. George walks away to mingle with the guys. All the men shake hands and say hello. Kenny is in front of him, they lock hands like they were throwing a boxing hook at each other, which turns into an embrace. Kenny looks across to Eva and the girls and then back at George.

"George, who is the lady?"

"She lives next door."

"Good looking lady! She's too tall for you though."

"Yep, she's tall alright."

"She has a great ass on her!"

"What are you, an ass magnet? What's going on with the ticket sales for the fund raiser?"

"The tickets have all been sold out. You'd know that if you turned up from time to time. Anyway, I want to ask you something."

"Ask, as long as it's not about the lady."

"What are my chances of having the hotel logo on the Liam's gown on fight night? I will pay for the gown and the logo. How much will it cost?"

"Nothing."

"What do you mean nothing?"

"How long have you been hosting fund raisers for Brendan's Boys Club at your hotel?"

"Ten years."

"And how much would you charge for the banquet room if it were for a private event for a night?"

"Three thousand pounds a night."

"Over ten years, that's thirty thousand pounds. The owner of the boy's club is Brendan, Liam, is Brendan's son.

I am one of the directors of that club. Without your help and support over the years, the boys club would be struggling. There is no price for you to have your logo on Liam's gown, understood?"

"I knew you'd say that but, I had to ask."

"I know. I'm starving. I know you are on a diet but, I'm going to get something to eat. Are you coming?"

Music is playing, wine is flowing, the guests are relaxing, talking, and eating. The tables are full of various meats and salads. Everyone seems to be enjoying themselves. Over at the BBQ there's a huge cloud of black smoke from the variety of meats cooking on the grill.

Brendan walks over to Eileen who is standing with Eva and Jackie.

"Can I get you girls anything? Some food or drinks maybe?"

Eileen smiles.

"No thank you darling. We will get around to that soon. Are you having a good time?"

"Yeah, it's great. Everyone looks like they are enjoying themselves, you've outdone yourselves again love. Please tell the girls thank you, and take some time to enjoy the party won't you."

"It's all perfect. We're enjoying ourselves and having a girls chat."

"No doubt all the boys are in the firing line. There's no girl chat without some kind of criticism of us men."

Jackie smiles.

"It would take me a whole year to fill in a complaint form for that great big lump Kenny over there."

"He is a good man."

"Ha! Try living with him!"

Just then police a car approaches and stops alongside the party. Two officers get out of the car. The young male and female officers take a few steps towards the party. Brendan walks over to greet them. Kenny and George stand next to Eva, Jackie, and Eileen. As they watch, the young male officer starts speaking to Brendan.

"Sir, we've had a complaint from someone."

"Complaint about what son?"

"Sir, don't call me son, I'm a police officer. Do you have permission to have this party here?

"It's a house warming party. No, we haven't got permission. Who the hell needs to get permission for few friends to gather outside their house?"

"Sir, I don't like your tone of voice. You look familiar to me, have we met before?"

Upon hearing this Kenny shouts.

"He's a criminal. Arrest him!"

Jackie elbows Kenny in the stomach.

"You shut up."

Just then Liam pushes through the gathering and stops next to his father. The officer recognizes him instantly.

"Are you Liam Murphy the boxer?"

"Yes, what seems to be the problem officer?"

"I'm a huge fan sir! I've been following your career since you turned professional, I watched your father as well, the great champ Brendan Murphy."

"My dad is standing right there, officer."

"May I make an unusual request sir?"

"Sure."

"Would you mind if I took a picture of the three of us together?"

"We're going to need few more people for this picture son."

Brendan gives a shout.

"George, Kenny, get over here."

George and Kenny move forward, the officer recognizes George as the corner man.
"You are George Williams the great trainer!"

"Yes, that's true." (Placing his finger across his nose, he pretends that he is scratching his nose but in fact, he is pointing at Kenny standing next to him.

"If you're looking for a criminal, I won't point any fingers."

The young officer smiles and passes his phone to his partner. The group assembles around the officer and his partners takes several photos.

"They are not going to believe this at the station!"

George steps forward taking the young female officer's hand, gently dragging her to stand with them for pictures.

"We are not interested in guys. We all fancy young beautiful woman in police uniforms. Are the stockings and suspenders standard issue for police women?"

The officer was obviously somewhat embarrassed but she smiled politely and replied.

"No."

The male officer then took several pictures of all of them gathered around her.

"I think everything is satisfactory here, no action will be taken tonight."

George steps forward again.
"I have a question for you."

"What is it sir?"

"On average, how long would it take to resolve an incident like this one?"

Eileen had been talking with Eva and Jackie but hadn't missed a beat of what's going on with George and the police officers.

"Oh, here we go, the man with the mouth is at it again!"

"I guess on average, about twenty minutes. It depends, sometimes these things can take longer if there's an argument and the people involved are uncooperative."

"Good! We want to argue. So, it will take a half an hour for you to resolve the incident."

"I don't understand sir. Why you would want to argue with me? I just told you the incident is closed."

"Come and join the party. Have something to eat. Even police officers have to eat right? After you've had a bite of food, you can both continue with your duties."

Kenny steps into the conversation.

"Do I have to call your Chief Superintendent and have him order you to stay and have something to eat?"

"Sir, my Chief Superintendent is in Spain right now celebrating his 25th wedding anniversary, the sergeant at the station can't even get in contact with him right now."

Kenny takes out his phone and looks through the contacts.

"We will see about that. Don't talk for a second."

"Harris, yes, it's me. Who else do you know that has a voice like mine? We have a little problem; I have two kids here a boy, and a girl, dressed in police uniforms with a squad car. They claim to be police officers. If they are in fact police officers, we'd like them to stay because George has invited them to eat BBQ with us at his house warming party. By the way you must have forgotten that you and Linda are supposed to be here too!"

Kenny then passes the phone to the young male officer.

The young officer responds.

"Hello."

The young officer's face becomes flushed as he is briefed by the man he is speaking with.

"Yes sir, thank you sir!" He hands the phone back to Kenny.

"Listen Harris, have a good time. Everyone here sends their love to the first lady. See you Friday night at the table."

"Sir I can't believe you have the private phone number for my Chief Superintendent. You guys are dangerous!" Kenny leans towards the officer.

"Son, we are criminals. We know everybody. Harris is a good friend of ours but he's a lousy card player. He wouldn't stand by us if we broke the law so, please join us and have something to eat, then you can be on your way."

Fiona moves close to Liam and wraps her arms around him. Liam puts his hand around her shoulder and kisses her tenderly on her head.

George looks at the young officers.

The female officer speaks.

"I am feeling a little hungry to be honest."

Kenny replies.

"Tell me which house made the complaint and I will go and smash their windows."

"Sir please, I've had enough excitement for one night."

They walk towards the table with all the food.

Eileen and Jackie are talking and referring to George.

"That man could convince a bear to have lunch with him!"

The police officers ate and wished everyone a safe and
happy night, then left the party, surprised, content and very
full.
The night had been one big celebration, but the evening was
growing late and everyone was preparing to clear up and
head home. The DJ had collected all of his gear and left. The
main group had cleaned up and threw away all of the trash,
there was virtually nothing for George to do but reflect on
the night and what a great time it was for all in attendance.
George went to finish saying good night to everyone.

Kenny had the small van that was from his hotel come and
collects the leftover food so it could be delivered to the
homeless shelters that he'd supported over the years.

Everyone embraced each other as they said their goodbyes.
George and Eva are both sitting in the quiet as things have
gone back to normal.

"Did you have a good time?"

"Yes."

"Good."

"I thought it was just you that was crazy but I was wrong. All your friends are crazy too!"

"I wouldn't introduce you to my circle of friends, if I thought they would not adore you. Crazy or not, they are all good people. Come on, let me take you home. Liam starts full training tomorrow. We have two months to prepare for the fight."

"How do you train a fighter? What do you tell him that inspires him to go out and win a fight?"

"First thing I unusually say to him is; watch out here he comes!"
Eva smiles and giggles.

"It sounds simple enough."

"It's a lot more complicated than that. My job is to study the opponent. By studying him, I'm able to know how he moves, how he fights, what he is like coming forward, and going backwards. Knowing how the opponent will respond when the other fighter is in trouble, and what is he like when he is tagged with a punch. That is how I make a plan to train Liam for each fight."

"So, you are the architect of the fight."

"My brain can beat the fighter after studying him, but my body is too slow. If it were me in the ring, I would get my ass kicked because I'm that slow physically. Liam is the boxer; he must take my advice when he goes into that ring with the knowledge and fight strategy, I give him. The idea is to win, that's my job. Both sides have the same theory of studying the opponent; it's the one who knows most that will win."

"What happens if your fighter does not stick to the game plan and he does his own thing in the ring?"

"That only happened once with Liam."

"What did you say to him?"

"No need for words, I gave him a hard slap!"

"You slapped Liam in a middle of a fight in front of all those people?"

"Better a hard slap from me, then getting beaten up by his opponent. I told him that if he has another round like the one, he had, and forgets the fight plan, I was not going to be in his corner when he came back."

"What did he do?"

"He followed the fight plan and went on to win the fight. He did complain to me after the fight, and asked why I slapped him so hard. I told him that the hard slap was for all the fights in the future, and to remind him that is that what's awaits him if he doesn't stick to the fight plan."

"Mr. Williams, are you really that cold blooded that you would humiliate your own boxer in a middle of a fight like that? Couldn't you just explain it to him?"

"Explain what? That the art of boxing is to risk your life by being able to hit and not be hit. Liam happens to be my godson; I don't want anything to happen to him. Liam is a family man with good values and morals; he is a credit to the community here in Brighton. I only ever want the best outcome for him."

"Is the man he is fighting dangerous?"

"Every man in a ring can be dangerous. This man has a ninety five percent knock out ratio. In twenty-two fights, twenty-one of them were by knockout. He only went the distance once. He is from Ukraine; he is not named **Andrei "The Savage Assassin" Yakov** for nothing!"

They arrive at Eva's door; Eva looks at George.

"Well, I wish you all luck on fight night."

"Thank you. Would you like to come to the fight? I can arrange it for you."

"I've never been to fight before. I think I might end up having an anxiety attack from all that stress of watching people beat each other up."

"I'm sure you are a good trainer, and I'm sure Liam is going to do great on the night of the fight. After all, he has you in his corner."

"Thank you."

"Thank you for the wonderful evening, I had a good time and managed to get through it without any panic attacks. In fact, I feel calm."

"My pleasure. I'd like to come in and stay the night and make passionate love to you, but I have an early start with Liam and the gang at four a.m."

"Why are you always trying and shock me with the things you say?"

"I'm sixty-three; you are sixty-five, what could possibly shock us at this age? We have both been around the block so many times and life has killed us so many times, what could shock us now? Nothing."

"You are right. Thank you for tonight. I'm glad I joined all of you. Good night."

"What no French kiss to say good night?"

"Mr. Williams."

"Yes."

"Good night."

Eva shuts the door in George's face. George hesitates for a moment and then walks away.

Eva leans back against the front door smiling. Wanting to laugh, she thinks to herself; That man is crazy!

For the first time in years, there is a sparkle in Eva's eyes and a big smile on her face. Shaking her head, she pauses for a second and then heads to the shower, it's been a nice evening and it's time for rest.

Chapter Five
Training Liam Hard

Training began at 4 a.m. Everyone is gathered and
stretching. At 4:30 they begin the five-mile jog. George,
Brendan, Liam, and a few other potential fighters from the
gym are all jogging together.

It is not a race against time it's a steady paced jog. Liam has
his head phones on listening to some music. Everything
seems so easy for Liam. Brendan and George always
complain about how out of shape they are and how it's
getting harder as the years pass.

They run two and half miles along the sea front, then two
and half miles back to the to the cars. Brendan has a new
Range Rover; George has his old VW Beetle from the
seventies. Forty years with this car and he cannot bear to
part with it. Everyone gets into the cars and they drive back
to the gym.

The gym is located in an industrial complex which gives it
the appearance of a warehouse. The gym is named "**Sweat
and Tears**.
Once inside, the lights go on and everyone begins the warm
up doing their usual shadow boxing for half an hour, slowly

building into a faster pace towards the end of that portion of the workout, George watches every move like a hawk.

The next part of the routine is sixty minutes on the heavy bag. After that, everyone hits the shower and gets ready for breakfast.

The group is going to Brendan's house to eat. Claire, Eileen and Fiona, have prepared the meal.
Everyone gathers around the big table and has a hearty breakfast. Afterwards the men rest before heading back to the gym for the afternoon workout.

At the gym, some local people from the press arrive and are there taking pictures and writing about the upcoming fight, they are joined by sports reporters and film crews who are making statements about the fight.

George has brought in three good sparring partners who all fight similarly to that of Liam's opponent. Liam is wearing his head guard and is in one corner with George discussing fight plans and across from them is one of the chosen sparring partners.

"You are a south paw. I want your right foot outside of his foot ok and you move to the right never to the left ok?"

Liam nods his head as George places the mouth guard in Liam's mouth.

"Ok touch them up and let's go!"

The two boxers stretched out their arms, touch gloves and get into a sparing position facing each other. Liam's right foot is outside of his sparring partner as George instructed.

Freddy Miles, "The Cut Man", arrives and walks over to George who's watching from outside the ropes. Freddy has been working with George for the past thirty years and is one of the best Cut Men in the business. Freddy looks and George.

"Here we go again."

"How do you feel Liam?"

"I feel great George!"

"Good I want you to keep popping that jab out and move to your right, make sure you keep your right foot outside his foot so you can move easily without tripping over his shoes."

"Ok George."

The bell sounds and they start sparring again. Liam throwing the jab sometimes doubling up, and then throwing a straight left while moving to his left.

After the match is finished George steps into the ring wearing a pair of boxing gloves, Liam is standing in front of him with his gloves on still sweating.

"Pay attention to what I say to you."

"Ok."

George gets into a fighting stance in front of Liam.

"Jab me."

Liam throws a right jab from the southpaw stance; George has his shoulder high and he rolls with the punch.

"Again!"

Liam throws the jab, again the punch hits top of Georges shoulder and he roles with the punch.

"Ok stop."

Liam stops and listens to George.

"As you can see, he has his left arm high to protect his chin and he rides the punch. When you throw your right jab first, it hits his shoulder and the power has gone out of it, then he rides the punch so there is no power left at the end of that jab. I want you to practice during sparring touching him on the shoulder with the jab and then come across with the left-hand lead. I don't want it straight; I want the left hand to be half hook and half straight. When he leans over to his right, you will be able to catch him flush with the half straight, half left hook."

"He is not an easy clean hit and he can take a punch."

"I know it's not going to be easy; no fight is easy. The split-second secret I'm going to show you now is going to make the difference on fight night ok."

Liam nods his head. George walks back a few paces.

"On fight night you are going to meet in the center of the ring and touch gloves as always."

George and Liam move forward and stretch out their arms and touch gloves as if the first bell has just rung and then they settle down into a fighting stand facing each other.

"Now, listen up. When I come out again and touch gloves with you and I'm bouncing around trying to settle into a boxing stance, when I stop you have a split second to let go of the left-hand lead as power punch."

"I got you."

"When you come back, you hit him again with the straight left power punch and this is how I want the pattern of the fight to go all the way. Tomorrow you'll start working on these few things during sparring."

"Ok George."

"I want that left hand leading every time your opponent stops bouncing and tries to get into a fighting stance. In that split second, I want you to let go of the left hand and when you land it, then you use the right hook to the body and finish off with a left hook to the head; and move to your right. Be sublime in there, I want you to confuse him. I want you to be stealth so that he never knows what's coming until it's too late!"

"Ok!"

Later in the early evening they are at Brendan's house watching Andrei **"The Savage Assassin"** Yakov's last fight. It shows Liam how he uses the straight right as a lead punch and how devastating he is, once he has his opponents in trouble. The fighter moves in to finish off his opponent and he is a devastating finisher. The referee steps in and stops the fight after his opponent is no longer in a position to defend himself. Yakov raises his hand is triumph.

"The right-hand lead" became famous in the fight with George Forman and Muhammed Ali. In the fight; "Rumble in the Jungle."
Ali confused Forman with that right lead. Time and time again, the orthodox fighters don't expect anyone to throw the right as lead this unsettled the opponent.

Liam watches the celebration on the screen.

"He is a great fighter."

"He is a good fighter, but not a great fighter. He wouldn't fair too well with one of the great fighters like Roberto Duran, Sugar Ray Leonard, or Tommy Hearns. The greatest skill a fighter possesses in the ring, is how cool he is at all times; how relaxed he is at all times, even under pressure."

Liam is still watching the screen.

"He has a sound chin and a devastating right lead."

"You're going to neutralize that from today onwards. You will train one hour a day throwing that straight left, and the straight half hook. The straight left is to unsettle him at all times by getting off first. The half straight hook is when you jab him and he leans to his right. This approach is going to be the key to winning the fight."

"I have my work cut out for me. I mean, I have to change everything in order to perfect this."

"You are going to throw thousands of these shots. You will practice on the bags, on the pads, and in sparring from now on until the fight night. You will work on this until you perfect it, until it becomes part of your mindset, until it becomes part of your armory.
You will work on this until it becomes second nature, habit, and totally natural to you on fight night. That's it for today; I'll see you tomorrow morning."

George heads towards the front door where Eileen meets and kisses him on the cheek. Brendan walks through the front door.

"See you tomorrow morning Brendan."

"Are you off George?"

"Yeah see you in the morning."

"Where is he?"

"He is in the front room keeping an eye on his opponent."

"Goodnight George."

Brendan heads into the front room and joins Liam.

"It's going to be one hell of a fight."

"Do you think I can do it dad?"

"That's a crazy question to ask me son. If I thought you couldn't do it, I'd never have signed you up for this fight. Are you having doubts?"

"No dad. I have the best manager in the world and I have the best trainer in the world. The rest is up to me, to follow instructions, train hard, and give it my all on fight night."

"You are a good fighter son. As you know, in order to become a great fighter, you have to put the work in. To become a World Champion is the beginning of greatness and even then, you have to work harder to keep that belt."

"I'm sorry for what happened to you dad. I want you to know how proud I am to be your son."

"What happened to me was not my fault. The corner man should have thrown in the towel, and the referee should have stopped the fight.
Neither of them did what they should have done, and as a result of their failures my opponent lost his life."

"You are a great champion dad. You could have gone on to defend your title many times after that. What you have done by hanging up your gloves in his memory, and leaving the game undefeated, that is truly honorable dad. You left the sport with your dignity intact, while honoring the life of your opponent."

"Well honor and dignity does not count for much when your opponent dies in the ring."

"I've never told you this before, but mum told me this a long time ago. Mum said; you gave half of your purse to his widow because she had two little children to bring up. That was never made public, only four people knew about that, yourself, mum, the widow, and George. I just want to tell you how proud I am of you dad. I'm not doing this to please you; I'm doing this because I love boxing. I watched you train when I was a kid, the smell of leather and sweat in the gym, have always been sweet to me. I knew I only ever wanted to be a boxer even though you did not want me to and you were against it, it's in my blood dad."

"I'm proud of you son."

"Thank you, dad. Kenny asked George if he could have his hotel logo on my gown on the night of the fight."

"What did George tell him?"

"He said yes. I said yes. I also said, that I would ask my manager so, I'm asking… What do you say?"

"Kenny is a dear, close friend. He's family just like George. Kenny has demonstrated his devotion to us in both words, and deeds. You are aware son, that without Kenny and his annual fund raising at the hotel; the gym would be struggling. I think it would be an honor to have his logo on the gown. Don't tell him that just yet. Let me talk with him Friday night when he turns up for the card game."

"Ok dad."

The whole week, Liam practiced what George had told him. Everything was as George pointed out. Each day it was becoming easier and more spontaneous to perform these tasks.

Chapter Six
Friday Night Card Game

Friday night card games were always held at Brendan's house. Brendan, Kenny, George, and Freddy, were all sitting at the table playing cards when Harris and his wife Linda arrived. Linda brought some Spanish wine for the girls, embracing Eileen and Jackie when she entered the house. They girls gather on the settee while Eileen poured some wine. Eileen then joined them with a tray of wine glasses and water and some delicious snacks. It was now time for girl chat and a wee bit of gossip.

Kenny looks at Harris.

"Well are you going to stand there all night? Are you in, or out?"

"I just got off the plane two hours ago, I'm still jet lagged but it's nothing compared to looking at your miserable face! Of course, I'm in."

Harris pulls up a chair and sits down and the card game begins.

George looks at Harris again.

"Jet lag ha! Maybe we can make some money off of you tonight!"

"To get money out of me, you're going to have to fight me for that money Williams."

Kenny joins in.

"We don't accept any euros on this table mate, it's all British pounds."
"You accept them at the hotel, why can't you accept them here?"

This isn't the hotel, it's Brendan's house and a private game."

Brendan sees the opportunity to wind up to Kenny regarding his hotel logo being placed on Liam's gown.

"While we are on the subject of hotels mister, what's all this nonsense about you asking to have your hotel logo on Liam's gown on fight night?"

Kenny was caught off guard by the silence in the room.

"What the hell are you talking about? All I did was ask how much it would cost? I'm willing to pay for it. I even offered to pay for the design of the gown. You don't have to shout about it, just give me a price and I will pay for it."

George steps in to defuse the situation.

"Hey! Brendan was just asking Kenny. There's nothing wrong with asking right? Let's calm down now, I've already told him yes."

"You said yes to him?"

"Yes, I did."

"You are the trainer. I make those kinds of decisions not you. What do you think we are running here; an advertising company for tourists?"

Kenny is totally shocked.

"Listen, just forget I asked ok! Let's just get on with the game."

Brendan takes the argument to another level.

"I'm not finished. If I say yes to you now, what is next a request? Maybe Harris would ask for Liam to be wearing a police officer's hat into the ring to promote the police force!"

"Hey, don't get me and my police force involved in your dispute. I've got enough problems dealing with the public."

Kenny is trying to compose himself and looks into Brendan's eyes.

"All I did was ask! If a stranger spoke to me like you just did right now, I'd knock him out! I'm tempted to knock you out and end this!"

Brendan steps back.

"You couldn't fight your way out of a paper bag, never mind about knocking me out, you great lump of jelly."

Kenny jumps up and knocks the chair to the floor.

"Get up! I'll show you whether I can knock you out or not! I will give you one punch and you'll think you were kicked by a horse."

Jackie interjects swiftly into the conversation.

"Kenny! You sit down for God's sake! You both sound like fifteen-year-old football hooligans!"

Brendon starts laughing uncontrollably. Soon George who was in on the joke, starts to smirk, and Harris breaks out laughing. Kenny knows he has been had and it was all a joke, he breaks out into a smile and calms down.

"You fucker!"

Jackie looks at Kenny.

"Kenny, watch your language there are ladies present."

George looks at Kenny.

"You've been told mister. Sit your ass down and let's get on with the game."

Kenny picks up the chair, sits down, shakes his head and looks at Brendan.

"It's our honor to have your hotel logo on the gown Kenny, there is no charge to you!"

"Thank you, Brendan."

Harris is watching Brendan and Kenny back and forth.

"What about the police hat?"

George and Brendon speak in unison.

"Shut up Harris!"

Linda is furious and shouts across the room to the table.

"Hey you two, don't you dare tell my husband to shut up or I will come over there and knock both of you out."

George glances in Jackie's direction.

"Oh my God, the mosquito has spoken."

"Williams, don't you talk about my wife like that or I will knock you out."

Eileen stands up and looks across to the table talking to all of them.

"That's it! I've had enough. Come on girls, let's go and have some supper and few glasses of wine. Maybe, with a bit of luck they'll kill each other while we're gone."

The gals all grab their purses and leave the house slamming the door behind them.

Miles the Cut Man speaks.

"All we needed here tonight was a referee!"

Kenny replies.

"Never mind about the referee, let's play cards."

Brendan deals a new round.

Just around midnight, George returns home in his VW.
Parking the car, he shuts off the engine and steps out.
George can see Eva sitting on the bench while Kimmy walks
around in the grass. It's another beautiful summer evening.
George walks over to the bench.

"Are you waiting for me?"

"I'm waiting for empathy."

"Well, I'm waiting for a miracle."

"It would be considered a miracle if you say something
without upsetting me Mr. Williams."

"I don't mean to upset you. I forget to filter out what I'm not
supposed to say and say the things I'm supposed to say."

George sits down next to Eva. Kimmy comes over wiggling
her tail at George. He leans down and strokes her.

"Do you want some loving, oh you want some loving yes sweet girl!"

"She gets all the love she needs from me."

"I wasn't talking to the dog; I was talking to you."

"Mr. Williams you seem to be having filtering problems again. Have you come here to provoke me?"

"I doubt anyone can provoke you."

"I've got some wine left over from the housewarming, shall I bring out a bottle we can have a little drink and relax?"
"Mr. Williams, I don't drink."

"What a shame."

"Why is it a shame? It shows that I have good morals."

"I was hoping that after few glasses of wine that you'd forget some of those morals and I could take advantage of you."

"It's time for me to go inside."

"Ok, I'll walk you home."

As they stand, there is second or two where they are both looking at each other, it seemed like forever before they stopped looking and began walking.

"Why is it that you insist on walking me home when you can watch me walk to my door?"

"Because I too, have good morals."

Eva lowers her eyes for a moment.

"Eileen sends her regards."

"Thank you, I thought she would have forgotten about me by now. How is Eileen?"

"She's good, as always. Such a great lady you know, just like you."

"There's nothing great about me Mr. Williams."
"Every man in the world would be envious of me if they could see a flake of what I see in you."

Eva is clearly moved by George's words of kindness. Emotions are running through her heart and soul while tears trickle out of her eyes, she turns away and composes herself.

"Thank you for walking me home. Come on Kimmy, time to go inside now."

She opens the door and Kimmy runs into the house. George remembers that he has a message for Eva.

"I almost forgot, Eileen asked me to invite you to join her and Jackie at the house next Friday night."

"Why? What's happening next Friday night?"

"For the past fifteen years now, a few of the local lads get together and play cards, on those Friday nights the girls have a girl chat and a bite to eat. Eileen would like you to join them."

"I see."

"Well, you have a whole week to think about it."

"Thank you. What are you doing tomorrow?"

"Tomorrow, nothing. If you want someone to do some gardening for you, I'm good for that. Maybe you'd like someone to cook for you? I'm good for that too! Last but not least, if you want someone to make passionate love to you; I'm definitely good for that!"

"I'm taking Kimmy over to Birling Gap and Seven Sisters, it's a nice place to have a picnic. They have steps leading down to the beach so we could walk the beach. Would you like to come with us?"

"I don't think it's a good idea."

"Why not?"

"I'm just repeating what you always say to me when I suggest something."

"Never mind about what I say to you. Is your answer yes or a no?"

"It's a yes."

"Good then, it's settled. I hope you have good manners to refrain for a day, from wanting to burgle my knickers."

"I was hoping you wouldn't wear any."

"Mr. Williams!"

"Yes, ok, ok. I promise I will be on my best behavior."

"I will make up the picnic basket and bring everything necessary."

"Don't you want me to bring anything?"

"No, just yourself. I will see you at mid-day out here."

"We can go in my Ferrari."

"Kimmy will probably have a heart attack in that thing by the time we get there."

"Hey be nice, it's not so bad, it's a collector's car"

"More like junk. I'll see you tomorrow at mid-day."

"Good night Eva."

"Good night Mr. Williams."

Eva enters her house, gently closing the door… she wonders what the hell she's doing.

Chapter Seven
The Picnic

It's mid-day, George walks out of his house and finds Eva outside. Dressed in a lavender colored summer dress and wearing a sweet straw hat with a rose on the ribbon, she looks absolutely charming. George is dressed casually in white cotton trousers and a striped shirt.

"Hello Mr. Williams."

"Hello Eva, you look fantastic."

"Thank you, you look pretty good yourself."

"Thank you."

George takes the picnic basket from Eva; they walk to the car. Kimmy follows the pair with her tail wagging happily. George puts the large basket down, reaches into the car and flips the seat forward for Kimmy to get into the car. Walking around to the other side of the car, he opens the door for Eva, she gets in and George smiles as he closes her door.

Taking the basket to the front of the car, George opens the boot, it's full of boxing gloves and pads. There's not enough room for the basket. George returns to the driver's side and flips the seat forward, placing the picnic basket on the back seat with Kimmy.

The only new thing in the car is the CD player. George inserts a CD. To Eva's surprise, it's a woman singing a Spanish song.
Eva knows the melody as it was made popular in the sixties in English and Spanish. Love songs have a way of staying in the memory.

"Do you speak Spanish?"

"No, why?"

"I'm just curious as to why are we listening to Spanish music?

"One doesn't need to understand a song as long as they are moved by the vibration of the song. I love Cumbias, Salsa, and Tango too. I also love French and Italian music. I love all kinds of music; what types of music do you love?'

"Well, I grew up listening to sixties and seventies music, so I have a love for mostly everything from that era."

"Me too! I find music fascinating."

"In what ways do you find music fascinating?"

"I guess music fascinates me because it can alter one's mood and feelings, at the same time it can make your imagination run wild with visions. I find this happens especially if it's a love song. If you have just broken up with someone you love, and you listen to those love songs it can bring you tears."

"I am totally aware of those songs."

"Me too, that's why I don't listen to love songs. I have enough going on in my head without feeling sad."

"So, you're a softie?"

"You know someone that isn't when it comes to love songs?"

"I guess not. From what I gather, you know about love and hurt."

"Yeah, I know about love and hurt, but I wouldn't say it quite as casually as you do."

"It seems that you've been really hurt."

"Hurt. More like, emotionally assassinated!"

"Were you married?"

"No."

"Have you ever been married?"

"No. All these questions, are you planning on proposing?"

"Mr. Williams, do you always have the smartest answer to everything?"

"No. I don't have an answer to you and me."

"There is no answer to you and me, we are just friends."

"Well, we could always be friends with benefits."

"I've never heard the expression "friends with benefits", I suppose there is some logic to that expression."

"Yeah, according to the young adults that use the expression, they are friends but they also have sex as friends."

"Mr. Williams, for two and a half miles I have heard nothing but sexual innuendos from your mouth. Is it possible that for the rest of the day, you could refrain from such nonsense? I was hoping to have a nice day today."

"Me too."

"They arrive at Birling Gap; it's a tiny hamlet consisting of a few cottages, an old red telephone box, a small red post office, a car park, and a busy hotel. The hotel is perched on the edge of the rugged Seven Sisters Cliffs just before you get to Beachy Head.

George stops the car by the car park and looks around.

"There's nothing here."

"This place has plenty of history Mr. Williams; I shall tell you all about it once we sit down to relax."

George parks the car, gets out, walks around, and opens the door for Eva, then flips the seat forward for Kimmy. Kimmy jumps out with her tail wagging with excitement. Eva puts

Kimmy's leash on while George removes the picnic basket. They walk towards and open field.

After a few moments' walk, Eva stops in the middle of the field. On one side there are the cliffs and sea that stretch out to France, on the other side; more fields and the three cottages.

George puts the blanket on the ground and then the basket. Looking around him, he then sits down on the edge of the blanket.

Eva joins him and opens the basket taking out the home-made sandwiches and a flask of hot coffee. Handing George a sandwich and some coffee they begin to eat lunch.

"The first time I came here in the sixties, I was a kid. There were eight cottages here, all built in 1878 for the Coastguard. The cliff has been eroding at a rate of about three feet a year, the other cottages that were here had to be demolished because they had become unsafe to inhabit and were hanging over the cliff. Life was all different then. This field was always full of families having picnic's and enjoying themselves."

"Life has a way of eroding all of us I suppose, not just buildings."

"Your tongue does not seem to be eroding fast enough for me Mr. Williams."

"There are two things on my body that work in perfect harmony, my brain, and my tongue."

"You mean you suffer from impotence?"

"Do you want to find out?"

"Certainly not! I've found that you maneuver your conversation so that your desired topic comes to the forefront of a conversation. You have an answer for everything Mr. Williams."

"It's not a bad thing is it?"

"I guess not."

"Why did you want me to come here with you today?"

"To use your words Mr. Williams, "I know a broken soul when I see one."

"We are always at the mercy of life. Life breaks us at times but there are flakes of genius, tenderness, love, joy, and happiness too. Life comes with problems, lots of problems, it's not something we can avoid."

"I hope I am not a problem for you Mr. Williams."

"Eva, having you around is a pleasure, not a problem."

"Thank you. To answer your question; I thought bringing you here would be a nice change from sitting on the bench outside the house. Also, I have not been here for years and I thought as friends; we could relax, talk, and get to know each other better. Is that such a bad thing?"

"No, it's a great thing and a thoughtful idea."

As they talk, more people begin to arrive at the field. Everyone wants to relax and enjoy the day. There are some older people, some young families with their children and dogs.
Some of the dads are playing football, others are flying kites with their young children, it's lovely really.

After sitting for more than an hour, Eva thought it she should take Kimmy for a walk along the beach.
She waited for George to return from taking the basket to the car before they made their way to the metal steps that lead to the beach. Eva starts to explain to George some history of the place as they descend down the stairs.

"These steps are new. They were just built in the last year. It's hard to believe that on the very steps we stand now, there used to be cottages that people lived in. The last thing to be torn down was the Birling Gap Boat House in 2014, another precious landmark lost due to erosion. The way things are going maybe the few remaining cottages will fall victim to the sea also. Don't forget that where we live is also close to the edge of the cliff, there is a good chance that the sea will claim our houses in twenty- or thirty-years' time."

"I never through about that."

At the bottom of the stairs, Eva takes Kimmy off of her leash, she happily runs along sniffing the ground with her tail wagging in the air. They are headed in the direction of the Belle Tout Lighthouse; it's above the cliff a little further along the Beachy Head Road. Eva continues her history lesson for George.

"Above here, a little further down, is the Belle Tout Lighthouse.
In 2010 it became a licensed bed and breakfast. The sunsets are spectacular from the lounge area at the top."

"Mr. Williams, would you like to sit down for a bit?"

"Sure.

The two sat on a large rock below the cliff facing the sea. The tide is now moving out and the edge of the sea is about twenty feet away from them.

In the distance is the English Channel, where large and small vessels make their passage to their destinations. The sea gulls circle above.

Eva appears very calm and relaxed looking out onto the sea. George on the other hand is getting agitated; he keeps looking around and up to the cliff top. Eva notices.

"What's wrong?"

"I'm just checking to make sure that this damn cliff doesn't fall on my head and kill me. I don't have the time to die now. I have a big fight coming up, we have a great deal of training to do before the fight, and I can't die before that!"

"You do love boxing, don't you?"

"It's been my life ever since I was five years old."

"How come you never got married?"

"A long time ago, I thought I had found my dream girl. We were happy for a while doing all the crazy things that foolish, young people do when they are in love but; it all ended suddenly."

"Why? What happened to suddenly end it all?"

"She died."

"I'm so sorry Mr. Williams; please forgive me I didn't mean to pry."

"It's ok; it was a long time ago. I don't mind talking about it. Only a few close friends like Eileen and Brendan, maybe a few others know, but I've never told the story to another woman."
"Mr. Williams, if it's going to upset you and I'm sure it will, I'd rather you didn't tell me the story."

"No, I am ok. It was a long time ago. I want you to know."

"Ok."

"We had planned to get married. It was a Friday when we went to the jewelers to pick out identical rings but we wanted them engraved; I was going to pick them up the next day.
That night we spent at home cooking together and watching TV cuddled on the settee. We went to bed around eleven, kissed each other good night and drifted off to sleep in each other's arms."

Eva can feel the emotion in George's voice, her eyes well up. George continued.

"I don't know what made me wake up at four a.m. but, when I opened my eyes, I knew there was something wrong. Her arms were still wrapped around me, her eyes closed; she looked like an angel sleeping in my arms. I couldn't hear her breathe. I tried so hard to resuscitate her but, she did not come around."

"I'm so sorry."

"There is a name for the illness, it's called, "Sudden Arrhythmic Death Syndrome, abbreviated, it's called SADS. It happens to young people unexpectedly in their sleep; we had no way of knowing this would happen. It was the saddest point of my life."

"I'm so sorry."

Both of them are now looking out to the sea and listening to the waves in a moment of silence. It's tranquil; the reflection of that time is sad but calm. They quietly stand and began walking back to the steps, up through the field and to the car.

The drive home was also quiet. Not much was discussed, just small talk about how lovely the day was, and how nice it was to see the sea from a different spot. George parked the car between the two houses near the bench and helped Eva to her door, carrying the picnic basket.

"The invitation from Eileen still stands for Friday night and it would make me happy if you were to come along."

"I will think about it. Thank you for the lovely afternoon."

"My pleasure, I'll see you soon."

George left Eva at the door and wandered over to the bench. Inside, Eva watched George as he gazed out onto the sea for a moment; he then turned around and heads to his house.

Chapter Eight
High Focus

On Monday morning at four thirty on the dot, Liam is at the carpark getting ready for his morning road work with his father and two sparring partners from the gym. George joins them with a sports bag in hand. In the bag there were two ankle weights for resistance, he hands them to Liam.

"From now on, and every day, you will wear these on your road work and then you will finish off with a hundred-meter sprint."

Liam takes the weights and straps them onto his ankle.

"Whatever you say George, you're the man."

"Make no mistake Liam; this is going to be your hardest fight."

"I know George."

George looks towards the sea and then at Brendan, then back at Liam.

"The pundits and commentators are already saying you don't belong in the same ring as Yakov."

Liam replies with an air of confidence.

"I've been reading the papers and watching all the TV reports, they all say the same thing, that with his ninety five percent knock out ratio, I don't have a chance.
I have only one answer to all of that; I have not spent twenty years in the gym getting here to be worried about someone else's record."

Brendan is beaming with pride as he looks at his son. George smiles.

"We are going to put twenty years of training and knowledge into twelve rounds of boxing to win this fight. I'm going to make sure you are in the best shape of your life for this fight. Now start running! I'll see you later at the gym."

Liam and the sparring partners begin their jogging along the sea front as Brendan and George watch. Brendan is feeling a bit emotional.

"He reminds me so much of myself."

"Yes Brendan, you were a great fighter, but it's his time now. He is going to be great like you. You of all people know my motto."

"Yeah I do! You don't train fighters to lose."

"Right! Now are you going to catch up with them, or you going to go and have some breakfast with me?"

"I'll see you at the gym later George."

George watches as Brendan jogs off to join the boys by the sea.

Later that morning, Liam began working really hard on the heavy bag, keeping in mind the instructions George had given him. First, the straight rights jab from a southpaw stance, then the half hook, half straight left, switching to the right jab.

Liam continues with a combination of hooks as if he is going for the body then switches up to the top as if he is going for the head with hooks and then straight left and right.

After the heavy bag, Liam went to sparring in the ring. He was moving like, Muhammed Ali and sugar Ray Leonard combined. Moving in with his jab, then a combination of hooks, and head shots. Liam then moved back out again, as the sparring partner throws a punch Liam is not there, he is out of range of the punch. George is watching Liam's every move.

When all the gym work was finished an everyone was leaving, a reporter from The Sky News entered the building with a camera man and a sound guy.

Brendan and George step forward to be interviewed by The Sky Sports TV reporter.

"Brendan, as Liam's manager and his father, why have you chosen to take on such a dangerous fighter as Andrei Yakov?"

"At this stage of his career, there's not much difference between the top five middle weight fighters in the world that includes the champion himself. Yakov is a good fighter we all agree on that. However, everyone in this camp believes we can win this fight and that's how we are going to approach it. We have a very solid game plan."

"Sir George Williams, you are a celebrated, world renowned trainer, that has produced countless champions of all different weights; you have been knighted and are in the hall of fame, how do you see this fight playing out?
We know that Liam has slick boxing skills, but Andrei Yakov is a knock out artist and known to be an animal in the ring with a ninety five percent knock out rate, are you not afraid that Liam could get badly hurt in there?"

"There are no easy fights. This is boxing, and there's nowhere to hide. If you want to become the World Champion, it's man against man in there. Of course, there is always a risk that the boxers are going to get hurt but that happens in any fight. I think they are evenly matched and it's going to be a great fight. Tell your viewers in America to tune in on fight night; it's going to be great while it lasts. Now if you'll excuse us, we have work to do."

The reporter responds to the camera as George and Brendan leave.

"Well, you've heard it here first! The great trainer, Sir George Williams said Yakov and Murphy are evenly matched, and it's going to be a great fight. There doesn't seem to be too much concern about Andrei **"The Savage Assassin"** Yakov's punching power in this camp. We will be updating you throughout the preparations from both camps. Now back to you, in the studio."

Friday early evening, George arrived home to shower and shave before the card game. Eva heard his noisy car pulling up and looked outside through the back window.

George is at the bench for a brief moment, then heads towards the house. Eva marches towards him with a box in her hands.

"Mr. Williams, this came for you today, the postman left it with me, it's a good thing I've known the post man for many years, as you've lied to me."

"I did? When?"

"From the beginning Mr. Williams. From the beginning! I can't believe you lied to me!"

"Will you get a hold of yourself and tell me what you think I've lied to you about!"

Eva pushes the box into his hands. George takes the box.

"What does it say on the box?"

"It has my name and address, what the hell am I supposed to be looking for?"

"You said your name was George Williams, the box is addressed to Sir George Williams."

"Oh that."

"Yes that! Why didn't you tell me?"

"I didn't think it was important enough."

"You've been to Buckingham Palace, and Knighted by the Queen and you didn't think that was important enough to tell me about yourself?"

"Well there's not much to tell really, it was a nice day, and a privilege to meet the Queen. To be totally honest, I was petrified that her hand might slip and she'd lop my ear off. Anyway, the parcel isn't for me, it's for you."

"For me?"

"Well, not for you, it's for Kimmy. It's a blanket, a little gift from me. I had Fiona order it on line, I'm not good with the internet and all that stuff, I'm old school."

He gently hands the box back to Eva.

"Thank you that was very kind of you. You didn't have to do this."

"I thought it would be a nice surprise for you."

"I was surprised alright, when I read your name on the box."

"Let's not dwell on that shall we? Right now, it's time for me to go get showered and shaved for tonight's card game. You do recall that Eileen asked me to bring you along this evening, right?

"Yes, I recall but I have to decline the invitation. Could you please give my regards to Eileen and tell her perhaps another time? Thank you again for Kimmy's blanket that was very thoughtful of you."

"Ok."

George walks away to his house.

One hour later, George is at Eva's front door. George rings the bell and waits.

"Is there something wrong Mr. Williams?"

"Yes."

"What?"

"How am I going to explain to Eileen that you declined her personal invitation?"

"Are you a man or a mouse? What do you mean how are you going to explain? Just tell her I'm busy, that I had made other arrangements."

"Come on now, she knows you are a semi recluse, she won't believe that. She's invited you to be friends with her, is that such a bad thing?"

"I'm sorry. I cannot go with you."

George looks at his wristwatch and then at Eva.

"Ok, I'll tell you what I'm going to do, it's seven o'clock now, I'm going to go and sit on that bench out here, and wait for you.

The card game usually finishes around ten thirty and I'm home by eleven."

"Please don't do that."

"I will sit out here until eleven, then I will go home if you won't go with me."

Eva shakes her head and closes her door as George walks to the bench.

Looking out the window, Eva becomes infuriated when she sees that George has not moved from the bench.

Twenty minutes later, Eva approaches George at the bench. Wearing a lovely white sweater and a black skirt, she stands waiting for George.
"You look great."

"Thank you; you are an incredibly stubborn man!"

"I've been told that before."

"We better be back here by eleven o'clock understood?"

"We will be."

George opens the car door for Eva, gets himself in the car and they drive away to Brendan and Eileen's house.

At Brendan and Eileen's, there are several luxury cars parked that belong to Brendan, Liam, Kenny, and Harris. George parks his car and then hurries to opens the door for Eva. Eva looks around noticing how huge the home was and noticed that there was a cottage on the property as well. George had mentioned that Liam, Fiona and the children lived there, this must be their cottage.

George can see Eva's apprehension; he stands next to her to make sure she is alright.

"Regardless of what happens to you and me, you will find a friend in Eileen and the other girls through that door. They are all my friends and they are the closest thing I have to a family, please relax and enjoy the evening."

"Thank you."

George motions for Eva to head towards the front door. The door opens and Eva and George are greeted by Eileen who welcomes Eva with a hug and a kiss on the cheek for George.

"I'm so happy to see you again Eva, please come in and join us."

"Thank you."

Eva and George look at each other for a second and part company. Eileen takes Eva to the Jackie and Linda who are having a glass of wine and relaxing, Eileen steps out to get Eva a cup of tea and returns quickly to join the girls.

George approaches the table where, Kenny, Brendan and Harris are seated. Harris is shuffling the cards getting ready to deal, he looks at George.

"You're late! What happened? Did she take too long to get ready?"

"Harris, shut up and deal me in."

Rubbing his hands together, George takes a seat.

A little while later, George looks over at the girls, they are all smiles and giggles. Clearly Eva is enjoying herself.

Eva, glances at the table and sees George looking at her. For a second there is glorious eye contact between them, then George turns away and continues to play cards. Eva returns from the moment and back to the girls who are telling stories about men.

The card game and the girl chat end on time and Eva and George say their goodbyes and head back home.
The street on top of the white cliffs was silent except for the sound of George's old car coming down the road.

Upon arriving home, George steps out to open the door for Eva.

"Thank you for a lovely evening, I'm just going to let Kimmy out for a few minutes to run around. Good night."

George doesn't speak as Eva walks to her door and calls to Kimmy. Kimmy came running, all excited with her wiggling tail trying to jump up at Eva. Picking her up in her arms Eva gives Kimmy a kiss.

"Hello baby, did you miss me?"
Petting her on her head she sets her down onto the grass.
George is still standing there waiting. Kimmy runs to George; he pats her on the head.

"Are you happy to see me? Yeah! Did you miss me? Did you miss me huh?

"What are you doing here?"

"I thought I'd stay and keep an eye on you. Think of me as a volunteer bodyguard here to make sure you're safe."

"It's perfectly safe out here Mr. Williams; nothing is going to happen to me."

"Well you never know, there are a lot of vessels going through the Channel tonight.
It only takes one captain with a keen eye to spot you through his binoculars; next thing you know, there's an invasion party to come ashore and kidnap you."
"Such a captain might be tempted thirty years ago when I was young, not now that I am an old hag."

"I don't see you like that."

Unsettled by the kind words, Eva loses control for few seconds and then she composes herself.

"Will you do me a favor?"

"What?"

"Would you just call me George? Mr. Williams is worn out."

"As long as you don't get any funny ideas."

"Me? Never! I only have good ideas for me and you like, making love, while making the walls and windows sweat from the passion."

"Are you trying to kill me George?"

"Wow! That's the first time you called me by my first name, and it was in the middle of love making!"

"We are outside on the grass we're not making love. God! If I have a few years left in me, making love would more than likely just kill me off altogether."

"Hey, making love has a lot of benefits you know?"

"I don't want to know about them. I don't want to talk about them. Kindly filter your thoughts; I don't want to ruin the starlight and tranquility I adore so much.

Eva calls to Kimmy and they walk back to the house. George waves goodbye and enters his house for the night.

Chapter Nine
Sea View Hotel Fundraiser

The banquet room is filled with influential people who reside in the local area. Everyone in attendance is there to raise funds for "Brendan's Boys Club" There is a boxing ring in the middle of the room, where sparring matches will take place during the event.

The women in attendance were all dressed in evening gowns and the men, in formal dinner jackets and bow ties, this has always been a very special event and everyone is dressed to the nines.

Brendan, Kenny, Harris, George, and Eva are all seated together.

Next to Brendan's table, is Fiona, Liam and the girls along with the special guest and the former World Champion Chris Eubanks. Chris holds a boxing record with fifty-two fights, forty-five wins, five losses and two draws. Chris is there to show his support and to help raise funds for the boy's club.

Brendan, Kenny, and Harris all look uneasy at the table as they wait for their wives. Fiona approaches Brendan.

"Eileen and the girls are running a little late but promise to be here very soon."

"How do you know that? We've been calling them for an hour and their phones are off."

"I have my ways; we girls stick together."
"As long as they haven't been arrested. That would surely cause a scandal!"

"When they arrive, you're might wish they'd been arrested."

"What the hell are they up to?"

"You'll find out soon enough."

Fiona smiles and returns to her table.

The Master of Ceremonies taps the microphone a few times.

"Good evening ladies and gentleman, my name is Chris Stevenson; I'd like to welcome all of you to the eleventh annual fundraiser for "Brendan's Boy's Club, "Where Future Champions Are Made."

Joining us this evening is the former World Champion; Chris Eubanks Chris will be helping to empty your pockets during the auction later this evening."

Chris stands for a moment while people clap and whistle. Chris then briefly raises his hand in the air in gratitude and takes his seat.

"Ladies and Gentleman, without further ado, we have a surprise for you this evening. The first act is not even on your programs, you may want to record this on your phones, and take a thousand photos.
Please welcome all the way from the Las Vegas appearing here for the first time at The Sea View Hotel, please give a warm round of applause for the mature, the sexy, "The Sensual Sisters!"

"Steamy Windows" originally performed by the great Tina Turner begins playing, Eileen, Jackie, and Linda step out onto the stage dressed in short skirts, high heels, stockings and suspenders.

Eva's jaw drops in surprise as she claps the girls on with enthusiasm.

Harris's face turns white as a ghost seeing Linda all decked out in her sexy attire.

The men appear to be in shock.

Once on center stage, Eileen is showing her provocative side with sensual strutting and mannerisms.

The guests all have their phones out and begin recording the show.

There are cheers and loud whistling as Eileen moves across the stage and Brendan happily joins in.

All the girls are now on stage, dancing very provocatively in time with the music. Kenny can't believe his eyes and is trying hard to stay focused.

The song continues, the crowd is going crazy as the girls continue to lip-sync and dance like superstars.

Eileen steps off stage with the spotlight on her and takes Eva's hand, dragging her on stage. At first, Eva resists but then she willingly joins along with the girls. George is watching and clapping in astonishment.

Eileen signals to the girls to follow her lead, as she pretends to be riding a horse with both hands in front of her, all the girls follow like back up dancers. Eva is clearly beginning to relax to enjoy herself.

Kenny and Harris shake their heads in disbelief.

The girls together are swaying and lip-syncing, hamming it up like mad as the crowd continues to go wild with excitement.

As the song finishes the place erupts! Whistles, cheering and an unexpected standing ovation! The girls saunter off stage waving goodbye to the crowd and blowing kisses to their husbands.

Harris pulls Kenny close.

"I should have called in reinforcements and had this place put in lock down so that all the phones and cameras could be confiscated!"

"Will you stop thinking about the law, and start thinking fun!"

Eva comes back to the table and sits next to George with an innocent grin on her face. George looks at Eva with his brows raised.

"Did you know about this?"

Eva shrugs her shoulders acting sheepishly.

Chris Stevenson returns to the microphone.

Ladies and gentleman that is one hard act to follow! Let's hear it for the ladies one more time!"
Another round of applause that lasts a few moments, then everyone quiets down for Chris's next announcement.

"Thank you! Over the next hour, there are some local amateurs that will be sparring in the center ring. All the amateurs have been training at Brendan's Boys Club and we are very proud and happy to have them here with us this evening. Once the sparring is completed, the much-anticipated raffle and auction will take place. Please enjoy these fine young men, and be prepared to empty your wallets for this wonderful club!"

The spotlight moves to the center of the room where the ring is. The bell rings and two young lads dressed in sparring gear begin to box for the audience. The young lads are watched closely by a referee who moves around the ring watching each move.

Five minutes later, Eileen, Jackie, and Linda walk to the table they all give their husbands hugs and kisses, then take their seats.

"Who came up with the idea to dance in front of hundreds of people, in stockings and suspenders?"

Jackie and Eileen both point a finger at Linda without saying speaking.

Harris turns and looks at Linda, she's wearing a cheeky grin on her face.

"You just wait until I get you home, I will determine your punishment then, but I believe I already know what punishment fits this crime!"

Linda cuddles up to Harris and in her sexiest voice she responds.

"Oh, I can't wait Chief Inspector!"
"Will you behave?"

The boys in the ring have finished, there is a big round of applause for them. It's time for the auction to begin. Chris once again takes the microphone.

"Ladies and Gentleman, it's the moment you've been waiting for, time to begin the Auction! The first item we have this evening is a football that's been signed by all the players from Brighton & Hove Albion Football Club."

The audience claps.

"Before we begin the bidding, I must tell you that Brendan Murphy Promotions has asked me to convey a message to you all here. When Liam becomes the World Champion, he will defend that title, right here in Brighton at the Amex football stadium."

Again, the crowd goes wild with whistles, claps, and cheers.

Chris Stevenson then holds up the football for everyone to see.

"Who will start the bidding at a thousand pounds?"

A man raises his hand, and then another hand goes up, raising the bid by one hundred with each hand raised.

"One thousand one hundred, one thousand two hundred, one thousand three, one thousand four, one thousand five"

George looks at Eva. His are eyes are sparkling with mischief.

The bidding continues.

"One thousand six over here, one thousand seven over there, one thousand eight over here, one thousand nine over there."

George grabs Eva's leg just few inches above the knee and squeezes it hard at the nerve point. Eva screams and jumps up. George jumps up shouting out

"Two thousand pounds for the lady."

Eva is looking around her nervously that she is now involved in the auction.

"Two thousand pounds! Are you trying to make me have a panic attack?"

George ignores her.

Eva whispers to George.

"I don't have two thousand pounds, how the hell am I supposed to pay for a football?"

"We have a two thousand pounds bid from the beautiful woman at table two. Are there anymore bids? Alright then, going once…"

"George I'm going to kill you!"

"Going twice!"

George stands.
"Two thousand five hundred pounds!"

"Two thousand five hundred pounds is the bid by Sir George Williams! Does anyone else want to place a bid? Going once, going twice, sold to Sir George Williams the great boxing trainer!"

Eva kicks George under the table.

Chris Eubanks walks over to George to deliver the ball. They shake hands and hug as they've known each other for a long time.

"George when are you going to come over to the house for a visit?"

"When you turn up at the gym. Chris let me introduce you two, Chris this is Eva, Eva this is my friend Chris Eubanks."

"So lovely to meet you Mr. Eubanks."

Chris takes Eva's hand and kisses it gently.

"C'est un Plaisir de te reconter Eva. I'm delighted to meet you, please call me Chris."

Eva feels a bit breathless for a second, George rolls his eyes.

"Chris, I'm donating the ball back to be auctioned off again."

"George, you have flair and panache man. Thank you!"

"Never mind about all that panache stuff just take the ball back."

Chris smiles.
"George, you're a cantankerous old beast! I'll see you at the gym soon!"
Chris walks back with the ball, handing it to Chris Stevenson and whispers in his ear.

Eva looks around feeling rather embarrassed; she pushes back her chair and excuses herself. Leaving the table, Eva makes her way to the ladies- lounge. George watches her, feeling sad because he knows he's upset her.

Eileen can see that Eva is rather upset.

"Ladies and Gentleman, it's my pleasure to inform you that the signed ball has just been donated back to us by Sir George Williams, you will all have another chance to bid again! Let's have a round of applause for Sir George Williams and his generosity!"

Eileen gets up from the table to check on Eva.

George feels embarrassed by the applause after seeing how Eva has responded to his little joke. George casts his eyes to the floor.

Eva stands before the large mirrors, her hair has fallen out of place, and she is breathing heavy and feels a panic attack on the way. Lowering her head for a few seconds, the door opens to the lounge and there is Eileen standing next her.

"Don't be mad at him, he did the same to me five years ago. I had a bowl of soup close to me and when I jumped up screaming, I accidently hit the bowl of soup! The bowl spun into the air splattering soup on everyone at the table, and landed on the mayor's wife lap."

"You are just teasing me to try to make me feel better."
"No! Honestly! Ask anyone at the table, they will confirm I'm telling you the truth!"

"He is crazy! I'm so angry right now, I feel like killing him!"

Eileen laughs loudly.

"What's so funny?"

"He does unexpected things like what he did tonight all the time, that's what makes him so special; he stirs things in people that makes them feel alive."

"Alive? I felt like dying out there, I wanted the ground to open up and swallow me up I was so embarrassed!"

"Don't give up on him. There will come a day that when you realize that he is the kindest, most generous man you'll ever know and you will understand on that day, that you are truly blessed to have him in your life.

Eileen fixes Eva's hair, and makes her look beautiful and composed again.

"If murder was legal, I would have killed him by now!"

"You like him that much that you'd want to let him off without years of torment?"

"He has no chance in hell of ever being anything more than a neighbor to me."

"Come now, the night is still young; we have plenty more dancing to do."

Eileen gives Eva a warm sisterly hug. Eileen steps back, looking Eva in the eyes.

"If I had the opportunity to recommend a soulmate for you, I would pick him every time; because I know he is the best guy in the world."

Eva looks at Eileen and can see the sincerity in her eyes and hears it in her voice. They leave the lounge and head back to their table.

The auction and raffle end with huge success and the party winds down for the night. Eva and George hug and kiss their group goodnight and leave the hotel; it's been a very long night for Eva.

It's nearly two a.m. as George and Eva arrive home. George parks the car and walk around to open Eva's door for her.

Stepping out of the car, holding her shoes, she hesitates for a moment before heading to her door.

"What a night!"

"It was a great night all around, I'd say."

Inserting the key in the door, Kimmy comes running to her.

"Hello Baby, Mummy is home."

Kimmy runs out the door as always.

"Thank you for tonight, it was wonderful apart from the knee grabbing."

"Oh that."

"Yes that!"

"Well that was just a bit of fun; you kept the girl dancing routine quiet from me though that was sneaky of you."

"It was worth it to see their husbands faces when they came out to dance."

"Well maybe next year, you can put on an outfit like that and join them."

"By this time next year, and no change to your behavior, I'm likely to have killed you ten times."

"Be nice, it could be a lot worse."

"How?"

"You could have some miserable guy living next door to you."

"At this late stage in life, crazy or miserable are not really that great choices for a woman to have to make."

Kimmy comes running, Eva opens the door for her and looks at George.

"Well that's my cue to say goodnight. Thank you for a wonderful evening George. Goodnight."

"Goodnight, have sweet dreams Eva."

Once in the house, Eva closes the door behind her; George puts his hands into his trouser pockets and walks towards his house.

Chapter Ten
Viral Video

Several weeks have passed since the fundraiser. Liam's training was going very well. Today was Friday, and that meant card night. Eva decided to tag along with George to Brendan and Eileen's house, for the evening.

Eva was every bit "one of the girls" now and felt really comfortable in their company. They laughed and exchanged views about life, talk about art and philosophy, and of course Eva's favorite subject, local history. Finally, she felt that she belonged. There was a new radiant warmth to her after years of personal isolation with just herself and Kimmy. Eva now had a tribe of her own.

Eileen turned on the TV and selected TrueTube (a popular site for music and video's) in the search bar; she typed in, "The Sensual Sisters", and then turned up the volume so everyone could hear.

The video had five million views over two weeks and had literally gone viral. The video begins to play, the boys are at the table and when they hear the music; they stop playing cards. Looking at the screen, Harris shakes his head, the girls start dancing together and they all sing along to the song.

"I should get the boys from cyber department to delete that video, it's humiliating."

"Harris, it would be even more humiliating if you and Kenny wore one of those outfits and someone filmed you dancing at the fundraiser next year."

"It's not funny Brendan. The hotel bookings have increased by twenty percent, they think the girls are part of our entertainment."

"What the hell are you complaining for? Your business is booming!"

"I'm not complaining George, business is good but the hotel is getting phone calls for us to give them details about the girls; they want to book them for shows for God's sake!"

"Well then, they are going to need a manager soon."

"George! Will you cut it out! It's no joke. There are comments under the video from kids wanting to hire them for birthday parties and stag nights! People actually believe the girls, OUR girls, are professional cabaret dancers!"

"It's not funny George, the other day I saw a guy wearing a T- Shirt with the picture of the girls, in the caption it read; "The Sexy, Sensual Sisters.""

"Well Harris, you're lucky Linda wasn't with you otherwise she would have signed autographs."

"What the hell are you talking about? It was Linda who spotted the T-Shirt and pointed it out to me!"

George laughs.

"It was funny that the guy didn't recognize Linda with her clothes on."

"I didn't want to tell you Harris."

"Tell me what?"

"There is a guy on the sea front with a stall selling printed T-Shirts of the girls."

"Will you stop winding him up already? Let's play cards already!"

The girls are oblivious to the conversation the men are having because they are dancing and having a great time together.

Liam, Fiona, Kate and Sophie enter the house. Liam has two huge pizza boxes in his hands, he drops one off to the men and Harris folds his cards and takes a piece, then the others grab some and they all enjoy a bite to eat.

Liam takes the other box to the girls, and puts it on the coffee table there near the drinks. Fiona joins the girls as they talk and eat.

Sophie walks over to Brandan and stands next to him; he picks her up and sits her on the table facing him; then kisses her on the cheek.

"Have you been a good girl?"

Yes, I have been a good girl grandad."

"Good."

"Grandad."
"Yes."

"Grandma sexy."

"What was that?"

"Grandma sexy."

"Who told you that?"

"Mummy."

"When?"

"When we watched the video of grandma, Auntie Jackie and Auntie Linda on TrueTube. Mummy said, Grandma sexy."

Harris smirks and turns away his head to stop himself from laughing out loud.

George leans in and kisses Sophie on the cheek; he grabs her by the hand and brings her arm close to his mouth.

"We have a bite."

"No bite Uncle George!"

"Are you a good girl?"

"Yes."

"Ok then, no bite."
Fiona, Liam, and Kate approach the table.

"Come on girls; say good night, it's past your bed time."

The girls hug and kiss Brendan, say good night to everyone and leave.

Brendan takes a bite from his pizza and under his breath just loud enough for everyone at the table to hear

"Grandma sexy."

All the men break out in loud laughter.

Eileen looks over at Brendan who is still laughing and smiling.

Eva is watching Eileen closely; she can see the love between the two of them. Then Brendan takes a second look at Eileen. His eyes are telling Eileen a love story, she is his world and he is hers. Eva then looks at George, he is looking back at her with a calm tenderness in his eyes, she holds his gaze for a moment or two then turns her attention back to the girls. There is a strange something happening for Eva, her feelings are awakened by the telepathy in the room.

Chapter Eleven
Eva's Confession

The drive home down winding lanes is quiet and calm; it is just before eleven p.m. The night sky is a beautiful black velvet color dotted with glistening stars that appear like diamonds to the eye. In the car a lovely Spanish song is playing.

Eva is relaxing and feels moved by the beautiful music, she looks out the window into the darkness then she turns back and glances at George.

"Have you ever thought about taking up Spanish lessons?"

"No why?"

"I was asking because are always listening to Spanish songs. I thought it would make perfect sense if you spoke Spanish then you be able to understand the words."

"It's not so much about the words or understanding them, it's about how the whole piece moves me, and creates all kinds of emotions and feelings that I then send out of my head and into the universe."

"I agree that it creates beautiful feelings in one's heart and soul."

George looks at her with a new curiosity.

"Those beautiful feelings you are talking about are either goals, or dreams in life."
"You're right. I have been craving fish and chips for the past three weeks, which has nothing to do with music or the universe; I'm starved at this moment!"

"Well then, let's go and get some."

Eva smiles.

Within an hour they had their fish and chips in hand and are strolling along the Brighton seafront under the blue lit arches. Eva and George are both eating with their fingers, happily informal.

"George, do you remember when they used to serve fish and chips in newspapers?"

"Of course, I do, those were the good old days."

"George, I'd like to tell you something."

"As long as you're not going to tell me you're in love with me its ok because my hands have oil on them, my breath smells of fish and the first kiss would be awfully fishy, not to mention, you'd have a handprint in fish oil on your ass and Harris would know right away it was my handprint!"

"I see you are having filtering problems again. Are you going to shut up and listen?"

"Yes."

The walk continues as the sounds of the waves hitting the shore make a beautiful soothing background for just this kind of conversation.
"Try not to interrupt me please."

"I'll do my best."

"My marriage was not perfect. People on the outside may have thought so and it was good in the beginning, but things changed. My husband was jealous and possessive, by the time I realized this, it was too late. He wasn't a bad man; he just didn't know how to love me the way I needed and wanted to be loved. Everything we had in the beginning died as did he, but not before killing my spirit in the process."

"I'm sorry to hear that."

"About three months after the funeral, I had a nervous breakdown and since that time, I've been living a solitaire life with Kimmy. I had the panic attack the first time we met, but I don't feel so nervous around you anymore, I suppose I'm explaining myself so that you'll understand the panic attacks and perhaps a bit about why they happen."

"Well you not being so nervous around me is a good thing isn't it?"

"Yes."

"I'm glad to hear that, and I want you to know that I ask nothing of you, except, to just be yourself around me."

"Like you do with everyone yourself George? I'm not sure I am that kind of crazy!"

"Yes."

"My mother would have cringed if she had heard some of the things you have said to me since we met."

"If you really look into my heart and soul, there is not a flake of badness towards you Eva, I enjoy being near you."

"Thank you, George. You do understand that you are still on trial right?"

"Oh yes of course I understand and I'm sure I will never be acquitted, not with my mouth."

"You'd be best to have your filtration system looked at and quickly!"

"If I totally filter myself, I'd be bored to death."

"Oh, I'm aware of how bored you'd be. Eileen shared a few secrets with me about you, but they all adore you despite your filtration problems."

"Really? How do you know that for sure?"

"I see the way you are with them, even the children adore you."

"You know they are the closest thing to a real family that I have, it's a mutual adoration."

"I wish I had a family."

"If you like, we can practice, we can't produce kids at this age but we can have fun trying."

Eva smiles and shakes her head as she takes a few steps away.
When Eva turns back to see where George is, he looking at her as if he were writing the perfect love poem, she smiles and turns back around.
George joins Eva and the two head back to the car.

When they arrive back at the house Eva lets Kimmy out and they both go and sit on the bench watching the many lights from distant boats and listening to the sound of crashing waves below the white cliffs. The entire night has awoken poem like thoughts in George as he looks at Eva watching the sea.

"Hope, the never- ending supply of love, the magic of believing in miracles, that chance that we can once again belong in a world, where everyone dies emotionally around us each day yet believing there is a better tomorrow, where we can feel again, love again, be alive again."

Is that a poem?

"No, it's just something I made up while looking at you."

"For someone with such a big mouth that can't control or filter himself, you are sensitive, and romantic."

"I'm nothing but a frightened little puppy, like most man when it comes to love."

"I never really had any luck with love."

"Well that makes two of us."

"Over the years I have seen so many people married or in relationships that always have something negative to say about their partners, why do you suppose that is?"
"I believe that some people have found that love is not perfect but as close to perfect as they can get so they accept the love they're committed to."

"You mean like Eileen, Jackie, and Linda?"

"No, they are settled in good marriages, long marriages. I was thinking more about Liam and Fiona."

"I thought Liam adored Fiona, at least that's what I see when he is with her."

"Yes, he does, when he first met her eleven years ago, he was just fourteen years old, she was like a whisper of a girl, so frail and thin. We were all having dinner at Brendan and Eileen's when Liam came into the living room and told us all that he had just met the girl he was going to marry and she was going to be the mother of her children."

"What did Eileen and Brendan say?

"None of us spoke for a few seconds; we just looked at each other in silence. I personally thought it was a teenage crush and he would be over it in a few weeks or months, we all did, but he thought different, he was completely serious. Eileen asked him how long they'd been dating, he said they weren't dating. This confused us even more and we definitely thought it was a passing fancy on his part, but for him, no other girl would do. As time went on, they started dating and he brought her to the house to meet his parents, he went and met her parents and next thing you know they were engaged and were married. Now, they have those two beautiful girls."

"That all happened quickly from what you're saying George. I'm sorry to ask but is she having problem losing weight or is there something going on with her health, you said she was so thin when they met."

"After she had Sophie, she started to put on weight and it's not because she eats too much. She finally found a doctor after three years and they diagnosed her with PCOP or "Polycystic Ovary Syndrome" a condition that affects a woman's hormone levels. She is now being treated properly."

"I'm so happy to hear that, she must have felt awful not knowing what was going on all that time."

"To be sure the treatments is making her lose weight, that's what the doctor said would happen, and it seems to be working, but it will take time."

George then nods his head in the direction of the house; they both stand up and walk towards Eva's door. Kimmy comes running her tail wagging as she zips into the house.

"It's been a lovely night George thank you."

"The pleasure was mine. Goodnight Eva."

Eva hesitates for a moment then closes the door behind.

Chapter Twelve
Training for Speed

It is another beautiful morning as the sun rises in the distance across the fields. George arrives at the white cliffs and parks on a steep hill. Liam had been following the car doing his morning road work he is sweating from his run as he stops near the car places his hands on his knees to slow his breathing a bit. There's a chill in the air and George could see Liam's breath as he exhaled. The deep red sun is showing its beauty as it greets the two on the Cliffside.

"George, what are we doing at this spot it's not our usual training area?"

George opens his trunk and takes out a big plastic bag with stuff in it and dumps it next to Liam.

"Here, you're going to need all of this."

Liam looks at the contents of the bag on the ground, there is a safety helmet that is used in American football, knee pads, arm pads, and leather punch bag gloves.

"George, I suppose I should wear this helmet on fight night the way he punches what are you thinking here?"

"Never mind about the night of the fight. Just put the gear on, it's time to work."

Liam starts putting on the gear.
George walks around to the front of the car and takes out two traffic cones and walks down the hill about fifty meters, he stops and places the two cones down the middle of the road about five feet apart, then walks back up the hill.

"I look like an idiot with this stuff on."

"Each morning from now on, you will be doing speed training, trust me; you are going to thank me that you are wearing that gear."

Liam is shaking his head.

"We will begin from here, you are going to sprint down to those two cones and when I say sprint, I mean fast as you can. Are you ready?"

"I'm ready."

"SPRINT!"

Liam starts to sprint down the hill towards the traffic cones, as he picks up speed, he can't keep his balance and falls over, rolling down the hill several times before sliding along on his stomach. He finally comes to a face down stop then, slowly gets to his feet. George is shouting at him from atop the hill.

"Come on let's go!"

Liam heads back up the hill again, turns, and looks down the hill.

"SPRINT!"

Liam sprints but this time, half way through, he loses his balance and falls again, tumbling several times before coming to a stop. Liam slowly gets to his feet.

"George, I'm going to break my neck if I carry on like this."

"If you don't do this, he is going to break your neck in the ring! Now get up here and go again, come on stop messing about!"

The process is repeated with yet another fall and rough stop. Liam is breathing heavy as he approaches the top of the hill again.

"Son, we have one month to go until the fight and we are going to do this every morning until you can run down this hill many times without falling. This is speed and coordination training; this is going to help you to win the fight."

"SPRINT!"

Again, Liam sprints but this time as he is halfway downhill a car is heading towards him, he trips and falls, the driver slams on the breaks stopping abruptly. Liam tumbles and rolls few times and stops right at the front end of the car. The driver is an elderly man, but jumps out of the car to see if Liam is injured. Liam assures him that he is fine and begins back up the hill again. The man returns to his car and drives off.

After several more attempts Liam manages to control his balance and stops falling. George watches each attempt and success with a critical eye. The training lasts half an hour then they stop for a break.

"That's enough for this morning, we begin again tomorrow morning."

Liam is a bit out of breath and nods in acknowledgement.

"Now I know why I needed all the padding and the safety helmet."

"There is a reason for everything, if you hadn't had the gear, you'd have broken your arms and busted your face, but this is one part of the training that will help you fight. All of this tortuous training before the fight is the foundation and conditioning for the fight, not a guarantee that you'll win."

"You don't think I'm good enough to win!"

"I never said that."

"You don't think I can win this fight, do you? You don't think I belong in the same ring as him."

"I've never said that."

"You think I'm doing this to please my old man, well I'm not! When I was a kid, I wanted to be just like him, a great champion. As I grew older, I saw the great things he has done out of the ring without throwing a punch. When dad opened the boy's club after retiring, he became an even bigger inspiration to me; I aspire to be a great man like my dad."

"Your father is a great man; his record out of the ring speaks volumes in the community. Your mum is a great lady, without her by his side he couldn't do half of the things he's done, together they are a great team."

"They are a great team. I'm doing this for me, Fiona and the kids. The three of them are my life."

"We all know that son."

"The other day, the four of us went to Brighton sea front, there were thousands of people there but she wanted to go and so we did. We stopped to get ice cream, as we were waiting, there were three women behind us around Fiona's age, one of them recognized me and told the other girls. I pretended I didn't hear, but then they started making fun of Fiona's weight, she heard them."

"What did you do?"

"I felt like turning around and slapping them but I didn't, instead, I looked at Fiona, leaned over and kissed her mouth as I told her I loved her. The three women saw and heard it."

"I'll bet they never saw that counter punch coming! Fiona is a great lady, and she is going to lose the weight now that she is on her medication. I know she has suffered a great deal as a result of putting on weight. I'm pretty sure she'd go through it all over again if the result of having those two beautiful daughters was the outcome. Fiona has your mother's virtues."

"I know. I don't think I'd be half the man I am if it was not for Fiona. Now, getting back to us, sometimes you say things to me that are so far of the chart that I don't know what the hell you are talking about."

"Well, if I say things to you that are so far of the chart, it's because I've lived it. It's called experience; it's called having paid the price to be where I am today.
 I'm giving you information that is off the chart so that you can use it, apply it and win your fight. I can't fight the fight for you, but I can show you how you can win it."

"You see, there you go again, talking off the chart. Just tell me in plain English what to do and I'll do it."

"You want plain English, here it is; the fight will be won in your mind long before the first bell rings."

"How in the hell am I supposed to win a fight without fighting? You're talking about psychology now to get into his head before the fight, right? Is that what you're talking about?"

"No, you don't need to be in his head to win the fight you need to be in your own head and you need to believe that you've already won the fight."

I'm sure there's logic to what you're saying or at least I think there might be, right?"

"Right! Remember these words always, the way to win this fight is you visualizing that the fight has already taken place, and you've won the fight. You must believe it, see it, live it, with all your movements, all your thoughts and feelings. You must see yourself as the winner in your sleep and in your waking hours. I said these words to your father when I was training him for his first World Title fight and you see how that worked for him."

George walks to his car and Liam joins him. Time for food.

Later that afternoon, Liam works on the pads with George. His speed is improving as he weaves and punches the pads taking jabs then combinations; slipping the punch then ducking and spinning under the punch.

George is in the ring with Liam and a sparring partner. George explains to Liam what he wants him to do when he is being backed up to the ropes.

"When he backs you up to the ropes and he is it pouring on, I want you to keep your guards up. Slip your right hand around his waist, pull him towards you, then spin him around onto the ropes and let your hands go with a combination while he is still trying to get his balance. Understood?"

"Yep."

"Let's go!"

George steps out of the ring and watches the sparring partner pressure Liam against the ropes.

"Spin him!"

Liam slips his right hand to the back of the sparring partner, pulls him forward and spins him around and pushes him onto the ropes and lets his combinations go.

"Stop, I want the movement to be natural and spontaneous, like one movement. You got that?"

"Yeah."
"Go again."

Liam starts again the sparring partner pressures him again onto the ropes, Liam turn and pushes him back onto the ropes and lets the combination of punches fly fast.

Chapter Thirteen
Kimmy

George is watching and studying Andrei Yakov, on the TV, outside it's thundering and lightning, as it begins to pour very hard, George steps to the window to see the lightning. Pushing back the curtain he sees Eva sitting outside in the pouring rain.

George runs out of the house with a blanket and hurries to Eva.

"What are you doing? What's happened?"

"Kimmy is gone."

"I'm so sorry. Come on; let's get you into the house."

Eva is soaked through to her skin. George wraps the blanket around her and they walk towards Eva's house.

"How long have you been out here?"

"I don't know."

"Why didn't you knock at my door and let me know?"

"I just wanted to sit alone for a while."

"You're lucky you didn't get zapped in the ass by lightning, I would have found you looking like Barbeque."

"Go into the bathroom and dry yourself off, then please put on some dry clothes; I'll put the kettle on and make us a cup of tea."

Eva heads to the bathroom without argument; George goes into the kitchen to put the kettle on and sees Kimmy in her bed. She looks like she is sleeping. George leans down, strokes her head, and then covers her with the blanket he bought for her.

Eva finally enters the front room wearing her night gown. Tears rolling down her cheek, her hair in a mess, she sits down on the settee with several tissues in hand. George brings her the tea.

"Thank you, George. You are soaked through to your skin. I've left a track suit in the bathroom for you, go and change or you will catch a cold. There's no point in the two of us dying from the cold."

"Shall I leave my shoes under your bed?"

"Instead of burying Kimmy in the garden, I'm going to kill you and bury you there instead."

"Be nice."

"You go do as you are told, and get changed."

George walks of towards the bathroom taking his tea with him. Eva has lots of framed pictures of herself and Kimmy together, she breaks down and stars crying again. A few minutes later, George enters the room wearing Eva's jogging outfit.

The arms are too long, the legs are dragging along the floor, he looks like a clown.
Eva looks at him and in middle of crying she starts laughing. George just shakes his head. Eva shakes her head trying not to laugh anymore.

"Only you could make an entrance like that, I was in the middle of crying over my Kimmy and you had to go and make me laugh."

"It's better to laugh then cry! Why do you have to be so tall?"

"Why do you have to be such a short- ass?"

"Good things come in small packages."

"I know. My Kimmy is gone now, what am I going to do?"

"If you are serious about burying Kimmy in the garden, I can do that for you tomorrow morning after training."

"Thank you, George."

Eva takes a sip from her tea, then stretches along the settee, placing her arm under head as a pillow.

George walks out the room and returns with a pillow and duvet. He gives the pillow to Eva she raises her head then lays it on the pillow. George gently covers her with the duvet.

Grabbing a blanket from the closet, he sits in the chair and covers himself up.

"Are you planning to stay the night Mr. Williams?"

"Yes. Only a coward would desert a friend at a time like this. Get some sleep please, do you want the lights on or off?"

"Off."

George reaches for the lamp and turns out the light. The rain, thunder, and lightning continue outside. Eva continues to cry.

"Kimmy was my best friend, I'm glad she didn't suffer and passed quietly in her sleep."

"I know and understand your loss. I will be leaving early morning because of training, but I will be back before lunch."

"Thank you, for being here. Good night."

"Get some sleep now, you need it. Good night Eva."

Eva weeps softly off to sleep; George closes his eyes, leans his head back, and gets comfortable to sleep for a few hours. The thunder is exceptionally loud and continues through the night.

In the morning, George quietly gets dressed so as to not wake Eva. Leaving the house, he drives to Liam. Liam has finished his morning jog, when George arrives on the hill and is dressed in all of his gear, doing sprints.

George watches, Liam is not falling even in the wet grass from last night's storm.

George leaves training after Liam's morning gym circuit and makes his way to Eva's house. Stopping along the way, George picks up a sweet Jasmine plant for Eva. George, grabs a shovel from his garden shed and heads to Eva's to dig a grave for Kimmy about half way down the garden along the side of the fence that separates George's house from hers.

Eva is standing close by watching as George takes Kimmy wrapped in the blanket places her in a small brown box and gently lays her to rest. After he fills the dirt back in, he points to the plant. Eva shook her head no and took a seat on a small gardening chair.

George steps back in silence with Eva looking at the grave; she produces a small piece of paper and begins to read from it.

"Thank you for the beautiful friendship over the years Kimmy, I know you have gone now, and yet, you will always live in the garden of my heart. I will always see you walking around the house, hear you bark, see you sleeping curled up in your little basket. I just want you to know, I will never let you leave the garden of my soul. Thank you for all the beautiful memories sweet Kimmy. Amen"

George looks at her and then to the grave.

"Amen."

Eva breaks down and stars to cry again, George gently folds his arm around her.

"Let's go inside, I'll make you some tea."

George didn't want to pry but was curious as to why Eva said no to the Jasmine.
"Eva, did you not like the Jasmine for Kimmy?"

"Yes, but not for Kimmy, I have a little statue I want to buy to place over her grave, the Jasmine will grow inside until spring, and then I'll plant it along the fence. It's lovely George and very thoughtful of you. Thank you."

Mid- afternoon, the doorbell rings. Eva answers the door to find Eileen, Jackie, and Linda. Eva has no words. Eileen hugs her tightly.

We are so sorry to hear about Kimmy, George told me this morning. This is no day to be alone, so you are coming with us. I booked a table for us at the restaurant we can have lunch and a relax with a good chat together."

"I have already had lunch."

"Rubbish, no one eats at the funeral, come on get ready your coming with us."

"Look at the state of me; I haven't even brushed my hair."

All three girls start rubbing their hair until they are all a mess.

Eva rolls her eyes at them and starts giggling, soon they are all giggling. Eva leans forward and hugs them all in one big sister hug.

Chapter Fourteen
Three Days until Fight Night

The last press conference before the fight is in London. The world media is there and it's being broadcasted live around the globe with the master of ceremonies Vincent Moralis.

"Ladies and gentleman we welcome you to this last press conference before the fight on Saturday night. For all those people who are watching live right now in the UK and around the world, I'd like to invite on stage now the boxers and their teams. Three men that need very little introduction, Liam Murphy, his trainer and hall of fame inductee Sir George Williams and his father, promoter, Hall of Fame Inductee the great Middle Weight Champion, Brendan Murphy!"

Brendan, Liam and George, walk onto the stage. All the men exchange handshakes with Vincent Moralis's and a brief embrace. The men have known each other a long time. Liam, George and Brendan take their chairs as Moralis continues.

Now ladies and gentleman please welcome on stage team Yakov. Moralis introduces the fighter Andrei Yakov, his trainer Bohdan Lyaksandro, and his manager and promoter Petruso Yevheniy. They all exchange handshakes with Moralis and take their seats.

Team Yakov is seated to the right of Vincent Moralis. There are camera's everywhere, reporters taking pictures and additional news film crews there as well.

Vincent Moralis continues after all the applause.
Ladies and gentleman and to all our viewers around the globe, we have two undefeated consummate professionals who are going to do battle on Saturday night to see who will challenge for the Middle Weight Championship Title of the World at O2 arena.

Back at home, in the main hall of The Sea View Hotel Brighton, Kenny is sitting alone smoking a cigarette while watching the press conference on the big screen. Moments later, Harris still dressed in his uniform, walks up to Kenny and looks at Kenny smoking.

"It's against the law to smoke in public places."

"Is this a raid?"

"I thought you didn't smoke."

"I don't, I only smoke three days before Liam fights and when the fight is finished, I quit again, sit down."

Harris pulls up a chair and sits down.

"A doctor once told my father when he stopped smoking that he was an addicted none smoking smoker, I guess that does not apply to you."

"I'm addicted for three days only, as I said, when the fight is over, I'm cured. Congratulations by the way!"

"For what?"

"You are going to be honored in the Queens New Year's list."

"How in the hell do you know that?"
"Linda told Jackie, and Jackie told me."

"Can't even trust my own family to keep their mouth shut."

"They are like sisters for Christ sake, three of them, no make that four now, with Eva joining the team. There will be no secrets!"

"What's the story with George and Eva so far? What's going on with those two?"

"How do I know? Ask the girls, they know everything!"

"I should arrest the three of them and lock them up, that's what I should do."

"What have they done now?"

"We were at Judge Anthony Parker's house for dinner the other night, his wife started talking about that video, she thinks it's great! I wanted to die; I nearly choked on my food as she went on about it!"

"What are you talking about? You should be proud; they raised a lot of money for Brendan's Boy's Club that night."

"They have also managed to raise a lot of eye brows in the community."

"What did the judge say?"

"He said he wanted to see the video himself."

"He has good taste."

"Those three women frighten me more than all the criminals put together in Brighton."

"They are talking about wearing police uniforms for next year's charity event."

"Kenny that's a bad joke. I have to get back to work; I'll see you Saturday when you pick me up for the fight."

"Righto, see you Saturday."

Harris leaves and Kenny returns his attention back to the big screen to watch Liam speak.

In Brendan's house Eileen, Jackie Linda, Eva and Fiona are all sitting around watching the press conference, Liam is talking.

"I have a great team around me. I have trained hard for this fight, and I am going to do everything I can to win this fight for my family for my fans and for me."

Eileen is so proud seeing Liam on the TV.

"Of all the things I have got used to, I can never get used to watching my baby fight; it was the same with Brendan."

After the press conference, Linda drops Eva off at home, its late afternoon Eva finds herself sitting on the bench alone; no Kimmy running around in the grass. Eva feels a strong tug on her heart strings.

George arrives a bit later and gets out of the car and heads to the bench. Eva is aware that he is there but does not turn to look at him.
"Hi, you're back."

George sits on the bench looking out at sea.

"It was only a press conference, were you expecting me to die out there?"

"Don't be so sarcastic, I just thought you wouldn't be back until after the fight Saturday night that's all."

"You're right, that is usually what happens, we stay at a hotel and turn up the next day for weigh in. And, the day after, we are at ringside for the fight.

"So why break the rules?"

"Trust."

"Trust?"

"Yes trust. It started with Brendan, he couldn't stand being away from Eileen and Liam that's why he had all his Title Fights here in London."

"Oh, I heard a lot of talk about being in camp. I thought boxers went to camp for few months."

"Usually they do so they are not distracted, but above all not to have sex with their girlfriends or wives. Sex weakens a man especially before a big fight or a game."

"How do you know they don't have sex when they are at home with their wives?"
"Trust and discipline."

"So that's how you make champions, and that's how you create history."

"It's a lot of shit. We are all trying to make a living that's all, the real champion of life is, life itself, and we all swim through this ocean of madness. There are no winners in life, life is hard for every everyone, life breaks us all, people disappoint us, people betray us, people hurt us, and as a result our fragile souls suffer. If we are strong, we find the strength to carry on even though we feel broken and disappointed."

"Two broken souls, sitting on a bench looking out to sea dreaming, who we can trust not to break us again?'

"Right."

"It's almost like they have been reading poetry to each other that was written for the first time. They just sit there looking out to sea, knowing they are finishing each other's thoughts.

"Did you miss me Eva?"

"No."

"That wasn't nice."

"Would you like a cup of tea? That's as nice as I am going to get."

"No thanks. I just want to sit here for a while and drink in your company."

Eva invites him into the house and is making tea; George is by the door that leads to the garden. Looking out at Kimmy's grave he spots a little statue of a Maltese. Eva must have picked it up when she was at lunch with the girls. It looks good there and the smell of Jasmine is wafting through the kitchen, over in the corner, is the plant he bought, safe from the cold and a sweet reminder to Eva of George's thoughtfulness.

Eva glances over to George and sees him looking at the grave, he turns and looks at her with calm understanding eyes, her eyes smile for a second at him and she takes some homemade biscuits and places some on the try with the tea and cream.

They sit outside in the garden at the small table for two Eva is emotional.

"One would never think that such a little dog could have such a big impact on someone's life. I had no idea it would hurt so much to lose her. I doubt I'd ever get another dog, it's too painful."

"It's too soon. Maybe, when you have healed from this; you will have a change of mind."

"I feel half dead as it is right now. I think it would kill me completely if I had another dog and lost it like Kimmy."

"Don't think about losing, think about giving, and think of how much love you gave to Kimmy, any dog would welcome that kind of love."

"You know what? It's not so much loosing Kimmy that hurts, it's all the beautiful memories, it remembering all the times it was just her and I."

George lowers his head, and gently nods in understanding.

Chapter Fifteen
Court

It's is seven a.m. and George's doorbell is ringing non-stop. It's Brendan and he's trying to wake George who answers the door half asleep.

"Come on, wake up! We have trouble."

"Brendan swiftly walks past George carrying a rolled-up magazine in hand. George closes the door behind him and follows Brendan into the front room.

"The world hasn't even woken up yet, how can we have trouble at this time of the morning?"

Brendan opens the magazine and shows George a page. George takes the magazine and starts reading about Fiona's weight problems, then looks to Brendan speaking calmly.

"Well, get a good lawyer and sue the bastard."

"Liam has already taken the law into his own hands. He went down to the magazine offices late yesterday afternoon, and punched the reporter in the face."

"If this happened late yesterday afternoon how come you waited to tell me until this morning? We have a weigh in at o2 arena at three p.m. today!"

"He was so mad when he got arrested that he refused to give his name and address to the police officers. When he didn't come home and his mobile was off, we called the police and reported him missing. Luckily, the young officer who came to complain about the housewarming party was on night duty at the station, recognized him and he got someone to come over to the house to tell us."

"Is his hand alright?"

"How the hell do I know? I haven't seen him yet. He's been in custody all night and is scheduled to appear in court this morning at ten."

"That doesn't give us much time; we have a three p.m. weigh in before The World Press."

"Let's just hope we have a nice judge and he does not remand him into custody until the trial."

"What the hell are you talking about?"

"He's been charged with Actual Bodily Harm."

"OH SHIT!"

George throws the magazine onto the chair and exhales deeply.

The two arrive to court, and are seated in the public gallery along with Kenny who was waiting for them, Eileen, Fiona Sophie and Kate.

Judge Anthony Parker is presiding. Liam is standing in the dock; the clerk of the court addresses him.

"Mr. Liam Murphy, it's been alleged, that on the first of August this year, you entered the premises of Brighton Ego Magazine headquarters and physically attacked Mr. Blackwell the Chief Editor of the magazine. You are charged with Actual Bodily Harm how do you plead?

"Guilty."

Judge Anthony Parker looks up at Liam standing in the dock.

"Mr. Murphy, I can see you have no previous criminal record which is unusual to say the least, do you have anything to say before I pass sentence?"

"Yes, sir I do."

"Please proceed Mr. Murphy."

"I love my wife and children Sir. I don't know Mr. Blackwell, I never met him before yesterday when I went to his office and confronted him. I wanted to know why he thought he had the right he had to say such ugly things about my wife. I love my wife, she is the most beautiful soul in the world, and she's the mother of my children and my life. Mr. Blackwell wrote such ugly things for the world to read about my wife, none of it true. Anyone who knows my wife will tell you she is an amazing person and not how she was described in this magazine. I did not hit him as he has accused me, I pushed him. I'm a professional boxer sir, and believe me, if I had hit him, he would have endured a knockout. My wife and family are my life and I'm truly sorry for pushing Mr. Blackwell, but I did NOT hit him your honor."

"Thank you, Mr. Murphy."

"Do we have the magazine as evidence?"

"No sir."

George stands up with the magazine in his hand.

"I have it Judge, and if I was him, I would have shot the bastard."

"Bring me the magazine please."

"What is your name?"

"George Williams."

"What is your relationship to this young man?"

"I am his godfather, his trainer, and longtime family friend. At three o'clock we must be in London O2 arena for the weigh in, he is fighting tomorrow night.

Judge parker takes the magazine from the usher and looks down at George is still standing.

"Mr. Williams this is my court room, I don't care what arrangements you have made for this afternoon or tomorrow night! Anymore outbursts like that from you, and you will find yourself in the dock. Have I made myself clear Mr. Williams?

George turns and looks at Kenny who shrugs his shoulders and turns and addresses Judge Parker.

"Yes."
Judge Parker is not amused.

"Yes what?"

"Yes Judge."

"Mr. Williams, you may address me as Your Honor or you may address me as Sir."

"Blimey, have you been knighted also?"

"Are you mocking me Mr. Williams?"

"No Judge, Your Honor, Sir."

Kenny then grabs George's jacket and pulls him to his seat.

Judge Parker then turns his attention to reading the magazine article. Andrew Harris, Chief Superintendent of the Brighton police then enters the room. Judge Parker glances up then rolls his eyes, and puts the magazine on his desk.

"I can see today it's going to be one of those days. Do you have a message for me Chief Superintendent Harris?"

"Sir, I have just come back from speaking with Mr. Blackwell, he has informed me that he has dropped all charges against Mr. Murphy."

Liam and his family exhale a sign of relief upon hearing this, but the Judge is not convinced.

"I see Chief Superintendent Harris. I assume you have a written statement from Mr. Blackwell to produce in court to confirm this."

"Your Honor, may I approach the bench?"

"This better be good."

Harris makes his way over to Judge Parker and whispers quietly so the courtroom cannot hear.

"What the hell is he saying to him Kenny?"

"Keep your mouth shut George or we will never get out of here. I called Harris to be here."

Harris continues the whispering. Judge Parker looks a bit shocked and begins to argue with Harris. Then things get super quiet as Judge Parker glares at Harris and then composes himself to address the court and Liam.

"Mr. Murphy, given this last-minute evidence produced by Chief Superintendent Harris, and given you and your family's standing in the community, and all of your charity works in the community; this court finds you not guilty. You are free to go."

"Liam come on, we've got to go to London pronto, we have a weigh in at three."

Liam and Fiona embrace as Liam tenderly kisses her on the forehead. They lock hands and head out of the courtroom.

Walking along the corridor inside the court building Kenny approaches Harris.

"What the hell did you say to him in there?"

"This is totally off the record understood? I told him that if he didn't let Liam go, that I was going to get a search warrant and raid his house for marijuana."

"The Judge grows marijuana in his house?"

"Quiet you! Medical marijuana only. He has arthritis and it helps with the pain."

"Maybe I should try some of that stuff."

"Don't push your luck."

Harries hurries along the corridor.

Outside, reporters are waiting for Liam to make a statement. Liam walks out holding Sophie on his arm and is still locked hands with Fiona. The reporters gather around him asking questions in a frenzy. Liam stops and hands Sophie to Fiona, kissing her on the lips, then addresses the reporters.

"My beautiful wife and publicist will answer your questions; I have to get to London for my weigh in at three o'clock."

Two motor cycle police officers come to Liam's rescue and drag him away one in each arm. There is a car waiting and they open the back door and bundle him.

George is sitting in the front with Brendan in the driver's seat. Harris reaches the window on Georges side and looks in the car at Brendan.

"You have a police escort to the o2. They will have you there within one hour in plenty of time for the weigh in, no worries.

Brendan looks at Harris with pride.

"Thank you for everything Harris."

"These escorts are not free! I will send a bill to your Promotions Company! Best of luck with the weigh in."

Kenny opens the back door and gets in sitting next to Liam.

Brendan looks back at Kenny.

"Where are you going?"

"I'm going to China! Now shut up, and drive!"

The two police escorts on motorbikes turn on their blue flashing lights and proceed away from the court house, the car with Liam and the men follow behind.

The escort is on the M23 motorway just outside Crawley heading towards London, the sign above the motorway reads; Gatwick Airport & London they pass quickly under the sign and continues the journey.

Chapter Sixteen
O2 Arena Weigh In

Outside of the O2 Arena, the World Press is awaiting the fighter's arrivals. Thousands of people have turned up for the weigh in. The Master of Ceremonies is Philip Sikes. As Liam and his team and Yakov and his team arrive the crowd gets loud. It's time for Philip to introduce the fighters.

"Ladies and gentleman, please welcome all the way from the Ukraine, he undefeated, number one ranked by the WBC, Middle Weight Contender of the World; Andrei, **"The Savage Assassin"** Yakov!"

Yakov climbs the stairs with his right hand raised and two fingers giving the "V" for victory sign, he is followed by his team, Bohdan Lyaksandro, and Petruso Yevheniy. Philip Sikes continues.

"And now ladies and gentleman please welcome from Brighton United Kingdom the number one ranked WBA Middle Weight Contender, Liam **"The Titanium"** Murphy!"

Liam makes his way up to the stage followed by Brendan and George. They shake hands on stage with the representative of the sanctioning bodies and people on stage.

The crowd is cheering like crazy! Boxing enthusiasts have come from far and wide and are anxiously trying to get video with their phones of the two contenders.

Philip Sikes continues.
"Alright fight fans, here we go! Tonight's much anticipated weigh in begins. This is the final eliminator for The World Middle Weight Title at 160 lb., or 11 stones 6 pounds, first on the scales; the fighting pride of the Ukraine, the undefeated, Andrei **"The Savage Assassin"** Yakov!

Yakov steps onto the scales lifting both arms and flexing his muscles, as a huge cheer is heard coming from the crowd, one of the observers clocks his weight at 160 lbs. and announces it.

Eva is watching the events unfold on her TV in her living room as Yakov steps off the scales and steps back to his side of the stage.

Philip Sikes continues.

And now ladies and gentleman, stepping onto the scales, the undefeated, number one challenger of the WBA, from Brighton England, Liam, **"The Titanium"** Murphy!

At the Murphy home Eileen, Fiona and Kate and Sophie are watching the weigh in together.

The crowd cheers loudly as Liam steps onto the scales and flexes his arms and muscles to show his lean cut body. The observers clock his weight at 160 lbs. and announce it.

Liam steps back and goes to his side of the stage.

"Ladies and gentleman, one final face of before the fight tomorrow night."

Both fighters take center stage and look at each other eye to eye trying to psych each other out.
In a sports bar, Judge Parker and Chief Superintendent Harris are having late afternoon lunch together. The weigh in is on the television.

"Harris, if you ever pull another stunt like that in my courtroom; I will have your house raided."

"On what charges?"

"I haven't decided yet, I will make one up!"

The Television announcer can be heard by the two men.

"That's the final weigh in for the big fight tomorrow night, but Liam Murphy is not the only member of that family who has become a celebrity here. We had an anonymous call today to draw our attention to Eileen Murphy, Liam's mother. It seems that Eileen Murphy and her two friends preformed at a recent boxing charity fundraiser, the video has gone viral on True Tube and has now had over ten million hits, we have it here for you this evening folks, look at this."

Judge Parker is watching the screen.

"Is that Linda?"

"No, she wouldn't be seen dead in a place like this."

Judge Parker can't take his eyes off the screen.

"No Harris, Linda is on the TV screen."

Harris looks at the screen and sees the girls dancing, he bites the pen in his hand that he was signing the check with.

At Eileen's house, Sophie grabs the remote control and switches channels to the news; Sophie calls out in a loud excited voice.

"Grandma sexy!"

Eileen looks at her with a smile.

"When did you learn to turn on TrueTube through the TV young lady?"

Fiona responds.

"That's not TrueTube, that's the National News."

Eileen watches for a second and grabs her mobile and dials Linda.

Linda is in an appliance store purchasing a new Television; she answers her phone seeing that it's Eileen.

"Hello there, what's new?"

"Linda turns on the National News now!"

Linda feels the urgency in Eileen's voice and asks the sales associate.

"Could you put the news on please? It's very important!"

The sales associate changes the channel to the news, Linda gasps.

"Eileen. We need to go into hiding."

Linda then shuts off her phone and tries to act unaffected. The sales associate recognized her immediately. "Would it be alright if I take a picture of us? I want to show my friends that I have met you!"

Linda shakes her head no and hurries out of the store, leaving the TV on the counter.

Later Friday afternoon, Kenny arrives at Eva's house with twelve long stemmed roses and a box of chocolates. He rings the door bell. After few seconds Eva opens the door, and sees Kenny standing there. Kenny shakes his head.

"I have been demoted from a hotel owner, to a delivery boy."

"Is he alright?"

"He is fine. Eileen has asked me to bring you over to the house will you come?"

"Sure, let me put these flowers in a vase; I'll only be a few minutes."

Kenny is standing next to a huge white limousine with black windows. Eva comes out the house.

"What's with the car?"

Kenny doesn't answer, he just opens the door and they both get inside. On the floor are three dozen red roses with more chocolates.

"No wonder you needed a big car."
"Those are for Eileen, Jackie, and Fiona."

"I thought the flowers I received were his idea."
"It was his idea. This is just covering all the bases; don't tell him I said that."

"You really like him, don't you?"

"I've never met a person that didn't like George, not even you."

Eva smiles at Kenny then looks out the window.

As they arrive at the front gate of the Murphy estate, Jack the gardener, is holding back all the press who have gathered there trying to get an interview with Eileen about the viral video. The limousine stops at the gate Kenny pops his head out the window so Jack can see him. Jack opens the gate and the car drives through.

"Jack, why are they all here and not in London to cover the fight tomorrow night? What the hell is going on here?"

"They are not interested in the fight; they are interested in the girls and that damn video on True Tube. It had turned the girls into celebrities!"

"Jack don't you have a shotgun to let of a few rounds off into the air? Maybe you can frighten them to leave."

"I'm the gardener Kenny, not a game keeper. If I had a shot gun, I would shoot you first! Now get the hell out of here and don't talk crazy like that!"

Kenny gets back in the Limo and the car drives of towards the house.

At the front door, Kenny gets out and holds the door for Eva. The front door opens and Eileen is there with Jackie and Fiona. They step outside. Jackie is wearing a hotel maid outfit.

The driver steps out and unloads the red roses and boxes of chocolates.

"Famous at last! What are you doing with the maid outfit on?"

"Kenny shut up! The hotel lobby is filled with reporters; I had to dress up like this to escape."

"Oh no! I will go over there and get them out."

"You can't get them out of there."

"Why not?"

"They are all booked as guests."

"I have a great idea."

"Kenny, I can't handle "crazy" right now, especially knowing the kind of crazy ideas that come out of that brain of yours."

"Let's all go inside and we can talk about it then."

They all step into the house.

George is in his hotel room watching an old boxing fight between Roberto Duran and Marvin Hagler for the Middle Weight Title of the World.
The bell rings for the third round, Reg Gutteridge is commentating as the two boxers square up in the middle of the ring.

"Remember that Roberto Duran has never been knocked out in eighty fights."

There is a knock at the door, George thinks for a second and then opens the door it, Liam is there in the hall.

"Hey kid, come on in."

Liam walks in and sees the fight on TV. He and George are watching as the fight is toe to toe.

"It was obvious that Duran was going to give it all his got, never been a gutsier fighter in the history of the game then Duran."

George takes the remote control and mutes the volume so they can talk.

"Is there something wrong?"

"No, I just came by to tell you that Freddy Miles is here and we have checked him into his room."

"Good."

Liam watches the Duran and Hagler fight for another second then turns and looks at George.

"I thought you be watching Yakov."

"I have studied Yakov a thousand times, in a million ways; I know the way he throws punches, how he breaths and what he's capable of. I know him well as his own corner."

"How do you rate Duran?"

"One of the best in the history of boxing. Period!"

"So, he is good as people say he was then?"

"He was better than good. When you look at what he has done in boxing, he was unbeaten as a World Lightweight Champion for 6 years; he successfully defended the title 12 times. Most boxers retire defending a title so many times. By the age of 29 many boxers would have retired, but not Duran, he moved up to Welterweight and fought the great Sugar Ray Leonard and won that fight!"

"That was a great fight; I watched that with my dad."

"Mike Tyson called it; "the fight of the century" and few would argue with him.

"How do you think the old man would have fared with him?"

"Your old man is one of the bravest fighters I know and if the fight could have been made between them, he would have fought him. I would have had sleepless night leading up to the fight. In 2002, Duran was voted by The Ring Magazine, as "the fifth greatest fighter of the last 80 years."

"I really think the old man would have been one of the greats if he'd never quit the game."
"He did not quit son, he did the right thing, for the right reasons. He left the game as an Undefeated Champion and sometimes to do the right thing; takes more guts then having the fight of the year or the decade."

"You're right George, I always felt like my dad did the right thing at the right time. I admire him for what he did. Anyway, it's getting late and I'm going to bed, I did not sleep much last night. I'll see you at breakfast George, goodnight."

"Goodnight son."

Liam walks out, closing the door behind him.

George picks up the hotel phone and dials out.

Eva is at home in bed watching TV. The phone rings.

"Hello."

"Hi."

"I thought you'd be busy in your room with a twenty- five- year- old at this time of night."

"I had three twenty-five-year-old's, that's a combined age of seventy-five, and they could not keep up with me! I thought it would be much more fun to bother a sixty-five-year-old, she'd know how to cope with me."

"I see."

"How are you? Are you alright?"
"I'm well thank you, and in bed."

"Every boy, dreams of talking to a beautiful woman in bed on the phone, I guess that makes me a lucky boy! Did you get my roses?"

"Roses? What roses?"

"You're not being very nice at the moment."

"Yes, I have them; they are beautiful, thank you."

"My pleasure. Do you miss me?"

"No, you have not been gone long enough for me to miss you."

"I won't have time to call tomorrow, I have a busy day. I just called to say goodnight."

"Good luck for tomorrow night."

"Are you going to watch the fight?"

"Yes, the girls have invited me over and we are going to the hotel to watch the fight."

"Good. I'll see you Sunday afternoon then, all being well."

"Ok."

"Goodnight Eva."

"Goodnight George, sweet dreams."

Eva hangs up the phone and cuddles down into her sheets, she's smiling and her heart feels light. The smell of roses has filled her bedroom, she is content and ever so quietly, happy.

Chapter Seventeen
The Sensual Sister's Press Conference

It's four o'clock on Saturday afternoon, the ladies have gathered at the Sea View Hotel. In the banquet room there are reporters lined up in the three rows of the seats in front of the stage. Fiona steps out into the middle of the stage facing the reporters, taking a deep breath she glances at Eva who is seated at the end of the first row.

"Ladies and gentleman, thank you for being here today. My name is Fiona Murphy and my husband is Liam Murphy, my father- in- law is Brendan Murphy. I am the PR manager at Brendan's Promotions. It's a pleasure to see you all here today in the same room that our charity fund raising event for the Brendan's Boys Club took place a few short weeks ago. As many of you know there was a video that has gone viral made that night and the three ladies in that video have joined us here for their very first press conference.
After the press conference, the doors will be open to guests that have purchased tickets to come and watch the fight live,

all the proceeds from the tickets today will go to Brendan's Boys Club. Thank you.

Ladies, please come on out. Everyone, please welcome, The Sensational Sensual Sisters."

The room is filled with applause as Eileen, Jackie, and Linda walk out and take their places on stage. Eileen is sitting in the middle, Jackie to her right, and Linda to her left. Eileen begins.

"Ladies and gentleman, thank you for being here. If I may, we are here to set the record straight, we had no idea the video was going to be seen by people all over the globe. I am a mother, a wife, and a grandmother, that is my job description. As a wife I support my husband and all the good work he is doing with the Brendan's Boy's Club. Brendan's built the Boy's Club to allow the opportunity for young teenagers to come in off the streets and away from drugs, knives and gangs. The mentoring at the Club is a way to give kids self-confidence, discipline, and purpose of in life. The video was done in fun to entertain our guests at the fund-raising event, nothing more. It was not done to draw attention to ourselves."

Jackie speaks next.

"Hello everyone, like Eileen I am a wife, and a business owner together with my husband; we own this hotel. For the past ten years, my husband and I have been involved in hosting a fund raiser for Brendan's Boy's Club, our primary goal is to raise funds to help the kids in the community have a safe place to go and learn. As Eileen has already stated, we did this act for a bit of fun to make the evening more enjoyable and entertaining. We are just ordinary house wives supporting our husbands for the good work they are doing."

Linda speaks.

"Hello everyone, I'd like to thank everyone who has seen the video and posted so many wonderful comments. I wish we had formed The Sensual Sisters twenty years ago; we could have made some money and have the fame at the same time."

Some of the reporters start clapping and whistling. Linda continues after a brief pause.

"The credit should not go to us; the real credit should go to Brendan. Brendan's Boy's Club is producing better lives for those youths, who aspire to be tomorrows champions; for giving them self-confidence and a true sense of purpose as I stated before. The credit should go to Brendan Murphy who established the club with his own money, with the help Sir George Williams who trains the kids alongside of Brendan and Liam.

Credit must also be given to Kenny and Jackie who each year put this great venue at our disposal, free of charge, to raise funds for the Boy's Club. We have received a lot of attention recently, and while it's all very flattering to say the least, we didn't do it for us but rather for our lovely community. Tonight, is a big night for Liam and we are here to support him, so thank you all for being here. Tickets can be purchased at the reception desk if you are joining us for this evenings fight. All proceeds will go to Brendan's Boy's Club. We hope to see all of you here tonight. Thank you!"

The reporters all start talking over each other trying to ask questions Fiona walks on stage and hold her both hands to quiet them.

"Please, gentleman, please."

The press quiets down.

"You will all get a chance to ask your questions, you there yes you, your question?"

"Do you have any plans to do anything like this at the next charity fund raising event?"

Linda stands up. "Is the pope Catholic? Of course, we plan to do more shows to raise money for the Boy's Club!"

Chapter Eighteen
Gloves On

In the O2 arena changing room, Liam is doing shadow boxing to warm up. Officials are everywhere. On the wall is flat screen showing the undercard fight going on in the arena. People are cheering and shouting at every punch being thrown. Pedro Mendez, the referee for Liam's fight enters the room to give last minute instructions to the fighter and the corner man.

In a small church in Brighton, Eileen lights a slim long white candle, and places it with other lit candles; crossing herself, she closes her eyes and starts praying for Liam and for the safety of both boxers.

In the changing room at O2 arena Chris Eubanks walks into the changing room, George makes a remark with a projected voice

"Look out everyone, the ego has landed."

Chris embraces Liam and they shake hands.

"You behave yourself George, only Reg Gutteridge is allowed to say those words, and I wish he was here to commentate on this fight."

"Me too, I hope he is watching from above and commentating to all the boxing fans in the great city in the sky."

He shakes George's hand and they embrace; he then moves over to Brendan shakes his hand and embraces him.
On the jumbo screen the final undercard fight has finished and the verdict is being read to the audience, it's time for the main event of the night. Freddy Miles places Liam's robe on him, The Sea View Hotel logo is on the back of his robe as they promised Kenny.

"We don't have to worry too much about any soft tissues son you have never been cut in a fight before."

The door to the changing room opens, in walks Fiona with Kate and Sophie. Fiona walks straight into Liam's arms and embraces him and holds him tight, Liam looks at her will so much love and holds her tight.

At the Sea View Hotel penthouse Eileen, Linda Jackie and Eva are sitting on a big couch watching the flat screen and listening to the commentary. In just a few moments the fighters will be making their way to the ring.

In the O2 arena changing room, one of the steward's motions to Liam that it's time to go. Liam crosses himself, embraces Fiona again, and kisses the girls and then leaves. Fiona asks one of the stewards turn off all the TV's so that she does not see the fight. Fiona is left alone in the big changing room with Kate and Sophie.

Kenny and Harris are seated in the front and begin to whistle and cheer as they see Liam on the big screen above; making his way to the ring with Chris Eubanks, George, Brendan, and Freddy Miles.

Freddy is carrying the bucket with all the things they need in the corner, there's white petroleum jelly, sterile cotton wool, dental swab sticks, a pair of blunt edged scissors, an ice bag, a roll of 1-inch zinc oxide plaster, a large quantity of soft bandages, and an eye iron.

George is carrying the white towels.

Master of Ceremonies Philip Sikes speaks to the audience.

"Ladies and gentleman, now we come to the main event of the evening. The first to come to the ring is from Brighton, the undefeated, Liam **"The Titanium"** Murphy! As Liam starts to walk towards the ring Kenny and Harris stand up clapping and cheering him on.

The Sea View Hotel main hall is full of Liam's supporters, they all stand and cheer as Liam enters the ring with his corner, and begins dancing around the ring shadow boxing.

Philip Sikes speaks again.

"And now ladies and gentleman would you please welcome to the ring the pride of Ukraine, the undefeated, Andrei, **"The Savage Assassin"** Yakov!

The whole place starts cheering, whistling, and clapping as Yakov enters the ring.

Eileen pours out large glasses of wine for each of the girls as Philip Sikes speaks to the audience about the record of the fighters and introduces the referee for this evenings contest as Pedro Mendez. Eva looks at Eileen.

"Eileen, maybe you should have taken a valium you look so stressed."

"I have already taken two, and said a hundred prayers."

Philip Sikes finishes of the introductions.
"Now I hand you over to the referee, Pedro Mendez for the final instructions."

Pedro Mendez calls both fighters to the middle of the ring with their chief seconds.

"I have given you instructions in the changing rooms, always pay attention to my command and protect yourselves at all times. Any questions from the blue corner?

"No."

"Any questions from the red corner?"

"No."

"Ok, touch them up and give me a clean fight!"

The fighters touch gloves and the corners and fighters return to their corners waiting for the first bell to ring.

Chris Eubanks sits at the front row next to Kenny and Harris.

In Liam's corner, George gives Liam last instructions while Freddy is putting some Vaseline on Liam's face.

"Deep breath son, relax, remember move to your right and don't forget the nanosecond us the left lead, as the lead to throw him off, don't wait for him get off first."

Liam nods his head, the bell rings for the first round and the referee ushers them into the middle of the ring with both hands inviting them to fight.

Both fighters are in the middle of the ring, both try and work out each other's strategies as they prod and poke and land selected jabs; both fighters are showing respect to each other and are aware of each other's punching power and skills.

At the hotel, all the local fans cheer as the bell goes off for the end of the first round.

Eileen exhales a deep breath and drinks some wine.

In Liam's corner, George is wiping the sweat from Liam's face, Brendan is giving him water to drink to wash his mouth and Liam spits the water into the bucket. Freddy is busy putting Vaseline onto Liam's face around the eyes, as George continues to give him instructions.

"Keep your right leg outside of his left foot, jab with the right, and move right, now and then drop that left lead in there to unsettle him; keep your hands up, relax come on now, scouting is over, pick up the pace, be first, don't let him dictate to you, walk him down."

Liam nods his head takes another gulp of water and spits it out into the bucket. The bell sounds for second round and George with both hands lifts Liam out of the corner seat almost shoving him to the middle of the ring, the two are back in the fight.

The pace of the fight has picked up from both fighters and no one wants to give ground as they exchange punches back and forth, it's turning into a great fight.
Jabs are thrown, combinations are thrown, but no clean shots are connecting as they are both defensive fighters and they block and slip the punches; heads are banging in there, the referee separates the fighters and tells them to watch their heads and invites them to fight again. The bell sounds for the second round to finish and they part and go to their corners.

George starts wiping Liam's face, Brendon gives Liam water to wash his mouth, then pours the water on his head, Freddy applies more Vaseline on his forehead and under his eyes George talking to Liam.

"Deep breath, deep breath, box as you are boxing, keep moving to the right be first, work and get out, time him when he is coming in, use your speed, come on, deep breath, deep breath."

"The guy can punch! I feel like I've been kicked by a horse."

"Liam, don't wait for this guy get off first, walk him down, use the angles, use your speed, and if he backs you up onto the ropes spin him and push away, then let your combinations go."

Seconds out, round three the bell off and both boxers meet in the middle of the ring, it's a fast start to round three and both fighters are exchanging punches in the middle of the ring. Yakov comes out with a six-punch combination driving Liam back, Liam composes himself and comes back with his own six-punch combination, driving Yakov back to the middle of the ring.

The commentator is excited with the speed of the third round.

"We came to see a fight, and a war broke out! Both fighters exchanging hard shots in the middle of the ring.

There is nothing to separate these two fighters, a hard right by Yakov drives Murphy back, Murphy comes back with a four-punch combination to the body and the head. What a fight this is turning out to be!"

Kenny, Harris, and Chris Eubanks are on their feet screaming and shouting.

"Go on Liam!"

At the hotel, Eileen and the girls are on the edge of their seats watching the fight.

Downstairs in the main hall, everyone is on their feet shouting and screaming as the fighters exchange hard shots in the middle of the ring.

"The countdown is on to end round three, and they are both throwing bombs in there, no man taking a back step, there is nothing to separate them; and there goes the bell and they continue after the bell! Referee Pedro Mendez steps in risking life and limb to separate them, what a great round!"

Both fighters go to their corners and water is thrown over their faces as they are wiped down with the sponge. Both fighters are breathing heavy and their corners are telling them to breath deep, both corners give instructions to the fighters as the bell sounds off and they start round four, where they left of round three with combination of punches coming from both sides.

Rounds five, and six, were the same, both giving all they have in the middle of the ring, fighting their hearts out. Both trainers shouting instructions from outside the ring. Round six ends and they both go back to their corners for the one-minute rest, they need so badly and to get further instructions.

"What a fight this is turning out to be! If this goes the distance, we might have a fight of the year contender. If this two keep up this rate of work… here we go again. Round seven, start of the second half of this fight and they are in the middle of the ring exchanging hard punches again! Yakov, has never been past six rounds before in the past three years, all his wins coming by way of knock out. Some critics said that Murphy did not belong in the same ring as Yakov, but so far; he is taking away the play from Yakov even though there's nothing to separate these two in terms of scoring. I make the fight even up to this point."

Rounds eight, nine, ten, and eleven are closely contested. As the bell goes to end round eleven, both fighters slowly walk back to their corners, they are both bruised and battered and tired now.

They throw water on Liam's face and sponge him down cleaning the blood from his nose. Freddy applies the cold metal ice pack to his left eye that is now swollen.

Across the ring, Yakov is also battered and bruised. His nose bleeding, his eye is swollen. He is given last minute instructions in Ukrainian by his trainer telling him this is the last round and he need to win this round.

In Liam's corner, he is breathing heavy, ice pack is on his eye, and he is being given water. Liam gurgles and spits it out into the bucket; George wipes his face down and gives him last minute instructions for the last round as Freddy applies Vaseline on both eyes.

"You need this round kid!   Go out there and give it everything you have!"
Liam nods his head in acknowledgement, catching his breath by taking in deep breaths, he calms himself for the next round.

"The difference between having another fight and facing the Champion for The World Title fight is determined by what you do in this round, now you go out there and kick ass."

Brendan leans in kisses Liam on the cheek and whispers in his ear

"I am proud of you son! You are a great fighter."

Liam is clearly touched by his father's words; he's made his dad proud and that means the world to him.

The time keeper shouts for round twelve. Liam gets to his feet, and the bell sounds.

Referee Pedro Mendez calls both fighters to the middle of the ring and instructs them to touch up. Both fighters touch gloves and they give each other a one-armed hug of respect. This is the final round.

"Look at this folk both fighters embracing each other, that's what this game is all about. When the fight started, they had no respect for each other but they both have certainly earned it now. The outcome of this fight depends on this last round."

Both fighters are in the middle of the ring both looking tired, but determined to finish the fight.

Fiona is still in the changing room with the children saying prayers.

Eileen and the girls all hold their breath as they watch on both fighters in the middle of the ring with the clock on the screen indicating that there is one minute to go.

Downstairs in the big hall people are cheering and shouting as boxers exchange punches toe to toe.

Kenny, Harris, and Chris Eubanks on their feet shouting and screaming for Liam to keep pushing.

"Some cynics said this was a mismatch when the fight was made, now they have to eat their words. This has been a great fight and a definite contender for the fight of the year. In my opinion, both fighters have shown great skills and have given it their all in there tonight. Ladies and Gentleman, we have ten seconds left in the countdown."

Both fighters are in the middle of the ring exchanging punches, the bell sounds and the round ends. The two embrace each other and tap each other on the head with their gloves. They take a breath to talk for a moment before the corner men all jump in and rush to their fighters to congratulate them.

After five minutes of celebration in the ring, both fighters appeal to the fans by raising their arms out to the audience. The audience responds with loud cheers and applauds. Philip Sikes takes to the mike to read off the score cards.

"Ladies and gentleman, after twelve rounds of boxing we go to the score cards but before the scores, how about another round of applause for these two great warriors who have given us a fantastic fight tonight!"

The crowd is loud and fills the arena with applauds, whistles, and cheering. They have witnessed an amazing fight and gladly show their appreciation.

Philip Sikes applauds with the crowd then reads the scores.

"Judge Juan Rodrigues from Mexico scores the bout 115 to 115.
Judge Raymond McAlester from the US scores the bout 115 to 115. Judge Phillipe Louis from France scores the bout 115 to 114.
The winner by a split decision is Liam Murphy!"

The commentator speaks.

"This fight could have gone either way with just a single point separating the fighters. Now we go inside the ring to get Liam's reaction to the fight as he speaks to Burt Stevens."

"Liam congratulations on your victory! You guys have put on a fantastic show tonight, there is already talk of this fight being a contender for the fight of the year! What are your views on the way the fight went and your opponent, Andrei Yakov?"

"When you are in the middle of the ring, it's not easy to say if you are winning or not. When a fight is so close as this was, it could have gone the other way, and I would not have been surprised. We both, gave it our all out here tonight. Can we have a round of applause for Andrei Yakov? Truly, a great fighter, he has my respect."

Again, the crowd roars with thundering applause and cheering.
Burt Stevens, pauses for a second or two and turns to Liam.

"This fight had everything in it apart from a knock down, what is your message to your fans and your doubters about you fighting for, The World Title?

Liam is now feeling the emotions of the night and the results of the fight.

"First, I want to thank my family, my mum and dad, my wife, and children, my friends, and all of my fans who have stood by me and supported me. I love this sport but without a great trainer, and mentor, I would not be here tonight; I'd like to thank George Williams who has been with me every step of the way, without his wisdom and knowledge this outcome would not have been possible."

"Liam, when you were in the corner before you came out for the twelfth round your father said something to you, would you like to share that with us? Also, what is your last message for Andrei Yakov on his performance tonight?

Liam motions to Andrei to join him and he obliges.

"Bert, to answer your first question, my father told me he was proud of me and said that I was a great fighter, that meant the world to me coming from such an incredible dad and a great Champion. My father makes me so proud for all the work he does for kids through his charity and gym."

Liam puts his arm around Andrei's shoulder.

"Andrei, my message is simple, in my next fight I will fight for The World Title and I will do my best to win that title. I will train harder and be even more focused. Tonight, I give you my solemn word Andrei, my first defense of that title will be against you."

Andrea claps. Both fighters embrace. The world of boxing lovers is going wild as Liam raises Andrei's hand to the sky in solidarity.

"Thank you all, for all of your support. God bless you, and have a safe journey home tonight."

Burt Stevens smiles at the two.

"What fantastic sportsmanship between these great rivals. They are two amazing fighters! There is no doubt the public will want a rematch as Liam Murphy has promised when he becomes the World Champion."

The crowd lets out another great cheer.

Liam enters the changing room where Fiona and the kids are waiting for him. Embracing Fiona, he kisses her softly on the lips and then drops down to his knees to kiss and hug Kate and Sophie. Liam's face is swollen and his eyes are puffed out. Sophie, gently touches Liam's face.

"Daddy hurt?"

"I will be very hurt if Sophie did not tell daddy that she loves him."

"I love you daddy."

"I love you too."

Liam turns to Kate.

"I LOVE YOU TOO!"

"I love you too daddy!"

The rest of the team walks in with other officials and reporters. Kenny, Harris, Chris Eubanks, and the doctor are there. The doctor checks Liam's eyes with a flash light. In a half hour they will go to a joint press conference about the fight.

Chapter Nineteen
Home

It's early evening On Sunday, the sun is making it's decent to the horizon as the boys arrive at George's house. George gets out of the car thanking Brendan. George walks towards the bench instead of going into the house.

Eva had heard the car and looked out the window to see George walking towards the bench, as he sits down; she lets the curtain fall and leaves the front room.

Within minutes, Eva approaches George with a cup of tea in both hands. Joining him on the bench she hands him his cup. Eva sits next to George as he is lost in deep thought gazing out onto the sea and the setting sun.

"Congratulations George."

"Thank you."

"I never realized boxing was such an emotional sport."

George nods his head.

"Did you miss me while you were away?"

George looks away from the sea and into Eva's eyes. George was filled with love as he searched Eva's eyes to see inside her soul. No words spoken, George leans over and softly kisses Eva on the lips.

Eva's heart is racing but not like it would with a panic attack, there is calm and secure feeling as she responds with a tender but passionate kiss in return. The kiss feels natural and has ignited a fire in her that had been out for decades. In that beautiful moment, Eva was alive inside and had no intention of letting this blissful, emotional feeling, subside. The two pull back ever so slightly and look lovingly into each other's eyes.

"I'm out of practice."

"Me too."

"Are you tired?"

"Just a bit."

"Let's go home and rest."

George looks at her for a few seconds, placing his arm around her waist, and hers around his; they walk towards Eva's house.

Once inside the house, Eva leads George into her bedroom.

"If you're too tired, we don't have to do anything; we can just rest and relax."

George leans forward and kisses her. Eva responds more passionately this time, the fire inside is now a full flame.

"I think I'm beginning to remember how this used to feel."

"I had hoped you'd say that, but this will be a memory, I will never forget."

Eva begins to take off her clothes; she is wearing a black lace bra and panties. George has taken off everything except his boxer shorts. Eva then pulls the covers back and slips into bed. George joins her and pulls her close to him. The kissing is incredibly more and more passionate with each passing moment. Eva can feel every fiber of her being igniting within her.

Without warning, George falls away to the pillow with a disappointed look on his face. Eva responds lovingly.

"Hey, its ok, I understand. Let's just rest and get some sleep, everything is fine, don't worry."

"Thank you."

George wraps her in his arms, pulling her to his chest, then kisses her forehead and closes his eyes. They fall asleep in the comfort of each other's arms.

At 2:35 a.m., Eva stirs awake. George is not there. After a moment, she gets out of bed and puts on her robe. Looking around the room she can see that George's clothes are not there, she heads to the window. George is on the bench. Eva slides into her slippers and quietly walks out to George.

"What are you doing out here?"

"I've been thinking about us. Ever since I moved here, the first day I met you, I began to lose myself, little by little. I have had a hard time focusing and concentrating, I'm forgetting things."

"Are you telling me that you have dementia?"

"No, I don't mean that at all. I've been crazy all my life."

"But you said you are forgetting things."

"I can't remember because you get in the way, I cannot concentrate or focus, because you get in the way; you have become a problem I cannot solve."

"Well if you feel like that, and being around me is so bad for you, I won't get in your way anymore."

Obviously feeling hurt and embarrassed, Eva turns to walk away. George grabs her by the hand and taps the empty space on the bench with his hand.

"Come and sit down."

"Just bear with me for a few seconds please. I have been thinking of telling Liam to get another trainer for his World Title fight, I thought about putting up the house for sale and moving, there's a million thoughts that run through my mind, all feelings of doubt. If I leave, the doubts will follow me and I don't know how to deal with it."

"I don't understand what doubts you are talking about. You are one of the most positive people I have ever met in my life; you're also the craziest guy I have ever known. What doubts are you talking about?
Can you explain all this so that it makes some sense to me, why I'm such a big problem for you?"

"I am in love with you."

"You're in love with me?"

"Madly in love with you, to the point that it frightens the life out of me. When we first met, right here, I never imagined I would feel like this, never."

"Well, it could be a lot worse."

"How? By running my mouth off, I thought it would keep us apart and keep me safe, that I would never reach this point with my feelings."

"I knew the reasons you were running your mouth of all the time."

"Really? You must be rather smart to have figured me out. Eva, I don't want it to be just sex between us. My doubts and fears are that you don't feel the same way about me, and it's killing me inside."

Eva takes his face into the palm her hands and moves forward, kissing him gently on the mouth while looking into his eyes.

"If you had said you did not love me, and I would have kicked your butt to France. Do you remember the first time we met here, I told you then that my late husband died sitting here on this bench?"

"Yes, I remember."

"When I looked out the window, and saw you sitting there alone, I nearly fainted that day. I thought for a second you were my dead husband, that's why I was so rude and angry. You reminded me of him; he was built like you and was roughly the same height."

"Are you trying to give me a complex? I'm drowning in love here."

Taking his face into her hands again, she looks him in the eyes trying to touch his soul.

"You are the closest thing to a perfect gentleman I've known and nothing like my former husband. You are kind, and generous, always treating me with respect while trying to use your charm to make light of the most difficult situations. Even though you have a filtering problem, you are a delight to be around, and I mean that. You are the unexpected and truly treasured empathy and miracle in my life. I'm madly in love with you Sir George Williams, and never want you to ever have any doubts about my feelings for you."

"Why didn't you say something before?"

"Every girl likes to be chased, even an old woman like me."

"The first time I saw you, I thought I was looking at God's handcrafted work of art, each time I look at you, all I see is the beauty that is you."

Eva kisses him tenderly.

"One more thing."

"What is it?"

"You are the last love story of my life and I want the magic between us to never end. I don't need or want material things, just you, just us, the way we are, in this moment, and forever."

"I will never let you down."

"I know."

"I want to wake up each morning in your arms, my heart filled with love, my soul comforted by your strengths and tenderness; and if one morning I don't wake up, I want you to know I have lived loving just you and the magic that is us."

"Thank you."

"Come, let's go home, we have unfinished business to attend to."

George kisses her passionately she responds by wrapping her arms around him. Eva takes George's hands and leads him to the house, hand in hand, he pulls her back a step, picks her up and throws her over his shoulder. Eva's legs are in the air, the sound of her laughter can be heard by the stars in the sky.

Printed in Great Britain
by Amazon